George E. Foster

Se-quo-yah - The American Cadmus and Modern Moses

a complete biography of the greatest of redmen, around whose wonderful life has

been woven the manners, customs and beliefs of the early Cherokees

George E. Foster

Se-quo-yah - The American Cadmus and Modern Moses
a complete biography of the greatest of redmen, around whose wonderful life has been
woven the manners, customs and beliefs of the early Cherokees

ISBN/EAN: 9783337195878

Printed in Europe, USA, Canada, Australia, Japan

Cover: Foto ©Raphael Reischuk / pixelio.de

More available books at **www.hansebooks.com**

SE-QUO-YAH.

SE-QUO-YAH,

THE

AMERICAN CADMUS AND MODERN MOSES.

A COMPLETE BIOGRAPHY OF THE GREATEST OF REDMEN,
AROUND WHOSE WONDERFUL LIFE HAS BEEN WOVEN
THE MANNERS, CUSTOMS AND BELIEFS OF THE
EARLY CHEROKEES, TOGETHER WITH A
RECITAL OF THEIR WRONGS AND
WONDERFUL PROGRESS TO-
WARD CIVILIZATION.

By GEO. E. FOSTER,

EDITOR OF MILFORD (N. H.) "ENTERPRISE."

Illustrated by Miss C. S. Robbins.

PHILADELPHIA :
OFFICE OF THE INDIAN RIGHTS ASSOCIATION, 1316 FILBERT ST.
TAHLEQUAH, CHEROKEE NATION: B. H. STONE.
MILFORD, N. H.: BY THE AUTHOR.
1885.

TO THE INDIAN ASSOCIATIONS
IN THE UNITED STATES,
COMPOSED OF NOBLE MEN AND PHILAN-
THROPIC WOMEN, WHO ARE ZEALOUSLY
LABORING IN THE CAUSE OF JUSTICE,
THAT THE REDMEN OF OUR NATION,
MAY BE FAIRLY DEALT WITH,
THIS LITTLE VOLUME
IS DEDICATED.

PREFACE.

Some years ago, the attention of the author was called to a brief but unsatisfactory item in a historical work to the "Cadmus" of America. A love of research finally induced me to collect from all possible sources the leading events of his life. In so doing the fact developed, that while many of our best scholars in the land are fully posted concerning the Cadmus of old, there are comparatively few who even know that an American Cadmus ever lived, and holds a high place among the great benefactors of mankind. It has been too much our custom to look at all Indians as savages, while in fact, there is much concerning them that is noble and even worthy of being imitated by a white brother. No Indian race has made such progress or possesses such a remarkable history as the Cherokee. Such history as theirs is not found in "Dime Novel" literature. Their achievements are of a higher nature: indeed, the truth concerning this people is more remarkable than the greatest fiction. In the preparation of this work, I acknowledge in the first place the very kindly assistance of many Cherokees, who are anxious to have the people of the States know more of the capabilities of their race. The records of early missionaries have been consulted for the early customs and beliefs of this people, and several who have spent years in the Cherokee nation have kindly given assistance. I am also under obligations to the writings of the Dodges, Drake, Schoolcraft, W. A. Phillips, C. C. Jones, Ramsey and others. Thus correctly as

possible around Se-quo-yah and his family has been woven the customs, manners
and the ever changing beliefs of the Cherokees for over one hundred and twenty-
five years. While this work is designed
to be the first of a series, it has been the
purpose of the author to have it complete
in itself, so that, on closing the book, the
reader will not only have a complete biography of Se-quo-yah, but a general idea
of the past struggles and present condition
of the Cherokee people. This work is
written especially for the enlightenment
of whitemen on the subject treated, yet
the author is not without secret hope that
his red brothers and sisters in the Cherokee Nation will be glad to have the story
of their benefactor freshly told. If this Biography shall raise to a higher degree, the
respect and sympathy of the more fortunate white man for his red brother; if it
shall encourage him more in the future
than in the past to aid the Indian races
in their struggles toward civilization, then
the work of the author has not been in

vain. That the day may soon come when Justice shall be the portion of all Indian tribes is the prayer of

Yours Truly,
Geo. E. Foster.

Riverside Cottage,
Milford, N. H.

July 1885.

CONTENTS.

—o—

CHAPTER I.

SALZBURGERS AND EBENEZERITES.

Cause of Emigration—Their Journey—Their Origin—Books of Devotion—Arrival in America—Founding Ebenezer—The Contrast with their Native Land—Appearance of the Town—Provisions for the Colonists—Final Fate of the Town—New Ebenezer—Its Rise and Progress—Present Desolation. *Page* 12.

CHAPTER II.

GIST, THE DUTCH PEDLER.

A Swabia-Franconia Arrival—Birth of a Baby Boy—A Pest to Ebenezer—The Unlicensed Pedler—Wooes a Cherokee Maiden—Purchases Her for a Wife—He Smokes and She Works—The Wigwam—Indian Hospitality—Around the Dinner Kettle—Sudden Disappearance—A Cause of American "Blues." *Page* 24.

CHAPTER III.

BIRTH OF SE-QUO-YAH.

Cotemporary History—Primitive Child-birth—The Guest Reception Seat Occupied—Visit of the Old Grand Parent—The Name—Cradle—An Indian Lesson—True Elements of success—The Religion of the Early Cherokee.   *Page* 37.

CHAPTER IV.

FROM BOYHOOD TO MANHOOD.

Boyhood pursuits—An important help to his mother Silver-smith—Black-smith—Trade-mark—Sacred Pipe—Debauch—Remorse—A Good Samaritan—Reformation, and Good Work among his People.   *Page* 49.

CHAPTER V.

FESTIVALS, GAMES AND DANCES.

Ball-playing—Conjurers—The Magic Seven—Conjuring for Health—The Health Roast—Tradition Keeping—Green Corn Dance—Chungke—A War Song.   *Page* 62.

CHAPTER VI.

A WARRIOR'S CONQUEST.

Warrior Making—War-dance and Song—Would make him dreadful—Fair Honors sought by the Cherokees—Se-quo-yah's Courtship—Marriage—The Early Cherokee Woman—Nature's Teaching He Dreams and She Works—A Family Disagreement Consequent.   *Page* 73.

CHAPTER VII.

STORY TELLING.

The Pisa described—Owatoga Dreams—Offers Himself as a Sacrifice—The Pisa Slain—Cherokees and Catawbas wage War—Hiwassee and Not-ley—Where the Waters Unite·-The Fawns—Success—Hiwassee's Warning—Flight—Reunion Marriage—Valley Home—The Story of Okefinokee. *Page* 87.

CHAPTER VIII.

AN INSPIRATION OF NATURE.

Se-quo-yah's Native Land—Nature the prime-motor of Genius—The White Prisoner—A Letter—The Mania to Solve the Mystery of the Talking Leaf—Se-quo-yah writes on Stone—A Derisive Laugh—Stung to Action—Dreaming. *Page* 97.

CHAPTER IX.

THE GREAT INVENTION.

The Voice of Nature—Picture Writing—Arbitrary Signs—Perfection of the Alphabet—Theoretical—The Scornful Laugh—His Perseverance —"A Prophet not without Honor"—His Final Triumph. *Page* 111.

CHAPTER X.

THE MISSION OF JOHN ARCH.

The Babe of Nun-ti-ya-lee—A Father's Care—Inseparable Companion—Expert with Bow and Gun—A Hero at Home—Ill Luck—Its Results—Life Empty and Void—Joins the Mission School—Career as a Student—Teacher and Preacher—His Journies—Translates Scripture into Se-quo-yah's Alphabet. *Page* 126.

CHAPTER XI.

THE KEY OF PROGRESS.

The Alphabet a National Institution—Suited for All—The Medal—The "Phœnix"—Its effect on the Nation—Circulation of Books and Tracts—The Rapid Growth of Civilized Ways—Laws on Scandal. *Page* 136.

CHAPTER XII.

CHECKS TO PROGRESS.

The Rapacious Whites—Speech of Speckled Snake—Troubles in Georgia—Unjust Laws—Driven out by the Guard—The "Phœnix" Suppressed—Emigration—Trouble and Suffering—Civil War—Their Alphabet now a Key to Progress. *Page* 153.

CHAPTER XIII.

SE-QUO-YAH, THE MODERN MOSES.

As a Teacher—Again a Dreamer—Would write a Book—Queer Expedition in Search of Knowledge Received in Honor—The Last Trip—Sickness—Death—Vision of the Past and Result of his invention—The Great Conception. *Page* 153.

CHAPTER XIV·

THE ABORIGINES ELYSIUM.

True to the Indian Faith—The Gates Ajar—Beyond The Gates—The Lost Race at Last—From Dust-Worn Ruts—Forgotten Benefactors—Among Indian Lore—The Little Book—Its Result—Wonderful Progress. *Page* 172.

CHAPTER XV.

A GRATEFUL PEOPLE.

Public Services—The Treaty of 1816—Treaty of 1828—The Literary Pension—Still Perpetuating His Name—Literary Societies—District—Bust, —Pictures—Testimonials of his People. *Page* 179.

CHAPTER XVI.

A LAW ABIDING PEOPLE.

The Cherokee Constitution and Government—Chief—Judiciary System—Courts—Jurors and Jury Trials—Laws on Treason—Murder—immorality—Intemperance—Recognition of the Sabbath, etc. *Page* 206.

CHAPTER XVII.

PUBLIC INSTITUTIONS.

Schools—Seminaries—Revenues—Asylums—P r i s-on—Churches, etc. *Page* 217.

CHAPTER XVIII.

THE FAIR LAND.

Location—The Surface—Productions—Statistics—Recuperative Powers—Missionaries—Never-the-less a Cherokee Civilization—Oconnostota's Prophesy. *Page* 226.

ADDENDA.

CONGRATULATORY.

During the researches of the author, he has had many words of encouragement from those acquainted with the result of Se-quo-yah's invention, and a few extracts from these letters are given below.

FROM REV. W. A. DUNCAN, CHAIRMAN OF CHEROKEE BOARD OF EDUCATION.

"You have selected Se-quo-yah as a special subject. He is worthy the pen of any student of human character. To my mind in the long chain of incidents that mark the development of the human race, no link can be found of purer gold than the life and character of that wonderful man. You cannot see him in his true light without placing yourself by his side, as he stood amid the disadvantages which environed him at the time he espoused the grand work of giving letters to his people. I feel much interest in the work you have taken in hand, and beg to express my sincere thanks for what is being done for the Indians by their friends in the States. I wish we could turn the Cherokee Nation up on edge as a map on a wall, so that people all over the United States could see us, each with his own eyes just as we are. I wish you success in your work".

FROM HUMANITY'S POET.

"I am glad the story of the Indian Cadmus is to be told in thy forth-coming book. I am very truly thy friend,

JOHN G. WHITTIER."

FROM GEORGIA'S HISTORIAN, C. C. JONES.

Se-quo-yah, the inventor of the Cherokee alphabet was a remarkable Indian, and I am glad to know that you are preparing a sketch of him."

FROM THE "CHEROKEE ADVOCATE."

"The truth is, most of the millions of intelligent Americans are not intelligent enough to make any distinction between

the red men whom they have been in-
strumental in extinguishing. They do not
know that there are civilized as well as
savage tribes of Indians, and Mr. Foster
has kindly and generously set himself to
the task of giving this information. It is
indeed true, that the Cherokee people
have a republican form of Government,
well administered—that they live in good
houses, cultivate farms, raise stock, fish
and hunt for recreation only, dress re-
spectably, educate their youngsters and
pay their own way—asking only not to
be interfered with, and particularly, not
to be exterminated. They have over one
hundred public schools, an orphan asylum, two high schools and fifty churches
with a population of twenty thousand.
They regulate marriage by law—and
allow no irregular intercourse between
the sexes, which are important facts most
American people do not know, but which
they ought to know. Mr. Foster in his
graceful, happy way tells these things.
Mr. Foster, is evidently a friend of Indians and humanity. Let us acknowledge
it and be thankful and grateful therefor."

FROM W. P. BOUDINOT, EXECUTIVE SECRETARY.

"I shall take great pleasure in giving you what information I can in relation to your subject at the direction of Principal Chief, D. W. Bushyhead. Se-quo-yah's invention made him a hero with his people and he now occupies among the Cherokees, by far the highest place among the celebrities of the red race. It is well that the American public should, if possible, be given a correct idea of Indian life, which varies of course in different localities."

MISCELLANEOUS.

Rev. Henry Morehouse, Secretary of the American Baptist Home Missionary Society writes—"I shall be very glad indeed to see your forth-coming book upon this famous man and the Cherokees. I have long wished that some one would write up the biography of that man and the history of his nation."

B. H. Stone, the Photographer at the seat of Cherokee Government writes:—

"I am glad if I can be the means, by assisting you, of making the people of

your country see us as we are. I wish
I could show to the world in one complete
photograph, the exact stage of civilization this people have reached. We are
glad, if there is one man in the States,
who is interested enough in our people
to perpetuate, for the first time after all
these years, in book form, the memory of
Se-quo-yah, the great benefactor of our
Nation."

L. D. Bailey, Editor of the "Cultiva-
tor and Herdsman," Garden City, Kansas, writes:—"I congratulate you on the
work you have taken in hand. Se-quo-
yah is a name to be honored as that of a
great man, who rose high above his sur-
roundings, and was first in his race in
inventive capacity becoming a Cadmus to
his people. The ever living verdure of
our great valleys watered and fertilized
by the river that flows past his western
home perpetuates his name and should
continue to hand it down for posterity to
honor."

Rev. Timothy Hill, Supt. of Presbyterian Missions, in the Indian Territory,
writes—"I am glad that your attention
is called to Se-quo-yah, for he is one of

the most remarkable men of the present
century. The invention of the Cherokee
alphabet was not only a philosophical
wonder, but was extremely useful. The
Cherokees not only used it because it
was convenient, but because it was an
invention of one of their number, and not
something brought to them by the white
man. The remarkable spectacle was soon
presented of a Nation completely ignorant of letters becoming at once a reading people, without the aid of schools
and without any regular class of teachers. Had the Cherokees been left undisturbed in their own home, they in all
probability would have gone rapidly forward in all arts and comforts of civilized
life. As matters now are, the Cherokee
language itself must, in the nature of
things, soon give place to the English,
and Se-quo-yah's alphabet and Se-quo-
yah's people will no longer be separated
from the great mass of the American
people, but blend into one and thus fade
away."

SE-QUO-YAH.

—o—

CHAPTER I.

THE SALZBURGERS AND EBENEZERITES.

Cause of Emigration—Their Journey—Their Origin—Books of Devotion—Arrival in America—Founding Ebenezer—The Contrast with their Native Land—Appearance of the Town—Provisions for the Colonists—Final Fate of the Town—New Ebenezer—Its Rise and Progress—Present Desolation.

About one hundred and fifty years ago, a little band of Germans, of the archbishoprick of Salzburg, in the circle of Bavaria, smarting from the stings of religious persecution, in order to escape from the oppression, arbitrariness and violence of a bigoted Popish Ecclesiastic, emigrated from the land of their nativity, as nearly thirty thousand of their countrymen had done

before them.*   Their objective point was
America.   Taking their wives and little
ones in wagons, they journied across the
country to Frankfort-on-the-Main; from
Frankfort they proceeded to the Rhine,
floated down the stream to Rotterdam,
and thence sailed to England, from whence
they were forwarded to America, by the
"Society for Propagating the Gospel."§

History speaks of these emigrants as being of the Bavarian proper, springing from
the Vindelici and the Boii, a people an-
ciently grave, loyal, faithful, constant in
their affections, attached to the ceremonies and faithful to the duties of religion,
ready to make any sacrifice that duty
might demand.   And this little band of

*The only form of religion, that was tolerated,
was the Roman Catholic, and in 1732, injudicious
and intemperate zeal was exercised to extirpate the
Lutherans. Leave was given them to withdraw, and
take their effects, and they were glad to do so, as
their persecutors became more severe.   Some went
to Protestant Countries in Germany and Prussia,
and a few to the English Colonies in America.

§Organized in 1701, the outgrowth of The Society
for Promoting Christian Knowledge, which was
formed in 1698.

worshippers, joyfully left the scenes of their
persecutions, rejoicing also that they were
thus afforded an opportunity of spreading
the truth of the Gospel, as they saw it, to
the Indians of the New World. They took
with them their Bibles and Books of Devotion and as they journied lightened their
fatigues with those grand old German
Hymns, which they were to make as precious in the New World, as they had been
to the people of God in the Old.*

From England they had a stormy passage of fifty-seven days and landed at the
port of Charleston, South Carolina. After
stopping there to recuperate for awhile
from their long, perilous and wearisome
journey, under the direction of General

*The Bibles accepted by these German Emigrants
were the Lutheran Versions, made up from the various editions of the Melancthon translations. Paul
Eber's translation was also accepted, and a few retained the translations of Leon Juda and John Pis-
cator, who were Calvinists. The unacceptable editions were those of Jerome Emser, John of Dieten-
bergh, the Newstad edition of 1588, the Hebron of
1595 and the Jasper Ulenberg translation in 1630.

The Hymns of Luther were indeed the battle cry
and trumpet call of the Reformation. The children
learned them in cottage, and martyrs sung them on

Oglethorpe, an officer of the English Army and member of Parliament, who had been granted by King George II., the region between the Savannah and Altamaha Rivers in trust for the poor, they proceeded in a body up the Savannah River about twenty five miles, and laid out a village which they named Ebenezer, as they said in gratitude to God for his guidance of them to a land of plenty and of rest from persecuthe scaffold. No wonder that these emigrants loved to sing the greatest of Luther's Hymns—

"Ein' feste Burg ist unser Gott."

It had long been the favorite psalm with the people. It had been one of the watchwords of the Reformation, cheering armies to conflict, and sustaining believers in the hour of fiery trial. What more appropriate words could they have sung on their tempestuous voyage than—

"A mighty fortress is our God,
A Bulwark never failing,
Our helper he, amid the flood,
Of mortal ills prevailing."

And how prophetic have proved the words of another stanza—

"And though the world with Devils filled,
Should threaten to undo us,
We will not fear for God hath willed,
His truth to triumph o'er us."

tion.   They passed Savannah on Reminis-
cere Sunday, by the Lutheran Calendar,
the gospel of the day being, "Our blessed
Saviour came to the Borders of the heathen
after he had been persecuted in his own
country."   It was on the morning of the
17th of March, 1734, that Mr. Van Reck
and General Oglethorpe, having left the
Salzburgers in tents went on and reached
the place designated for the future home
of the emigrants. It was four miles below
the present town of Springfield, Georgia,
sterile and unattractive.* From the earliest known history of the Salzburgers, as
the descendants of the Vindelici and the
Boii, they had lived on mountains or in
the valleys between the hills, and now for
the first time they were in a country total-
ly unlike that in which they or their ancestors had dwelt.   To the eye of the
Commissary, however, tired of the sea and
wearied with persecutions, it appeared a
blessed spot, redolent of sweet hopes,
bright promise and charming repose.   In
his journal he thus described the place:—
"A little rivulet, whose waters are as clear

*History of Georgia. C. C. Jones.

as Crystal glides by the town; another runs
through it and both fall into the Ebenezer.
The Woods are not as thick as in other
Places. The sweet Zephyrs preserve a
delicious coolness, not-with-standing the
scorching Beams of the Sun. There are
very fine Meadows in which a great quan_
tity of Hay may be made with very lit_
tle Pains. There are also Hillocks very fit
for Vines. The Cedar, Cypress and Oak
make a greater part of the Woods. The
earth is so fertile that it will bring forth
anything that can be sown or planted in
it, whether Fruit, Herbs or Trees."

The Salzburgers at once began to clear
the land and to build their shanties. They
were not left without some assurance of assistance. Before leaving England, the Society for promoting Christian Knowledge
had agreed to a series of articles in their
behalf. Not only had they agreed to pay
the leading expenses of the voyage, but
also to such as required an allowance was
to be made for tools, and on their arrival
in Georgia, each family was to have pro-
vision given them gratis till they could
make a harvest, and seed was to be giv-

en them sufficient to sow the land that they on the first year would make ready for the sowing. By the agreement on the part of the Salzburgers, they were to aid each other in preparing the land, and having at once set to work, by the first of May, they had made a goodly clearing. On that day, they received from Savannah ten cows, and calves and ten casks full of all kinds of seeds. The condition of the Colony was however extremely wretched, so much so that even the Indians, commiserating their poverty frequently sent them deer. For the first year, they depended almost entirely on the charity of the trustees. They had few tools to work with, and fewer mechanics. The rude houses which they had constructed were poor protection from the weather; the water proved bad and the soil proved anything but good and considerable sickness followed. The following year, fifty-seven more emigrants were added to the Colony, and among them were several mechanics, so that the work of building proceeded more satisfactorily.

In 1736, the settlement numbered two-hundred people, but the greatest dissatisfaction prevailed, and there was reason for their discontent. A conference was held, and leave was given the settlers to remove their town, which they commenced to do without delay. The removal took scarcely two years, and in June 1738, old Ebenezer had degenerated into a cowpen. "Thus early," says Jones, Georgia's well-known historian, "did old Ebenezer take its place among the lost towns of Georgia. Its life of sorrows, of ill-founded hope and sure disappointment was measured by scarcely more than two years, and its frail memories were speedily lost amid the sighs and shadows of the monotenous pines which environed the place." Not a trace of old Ebenezer can be found to day.

The village of New Ebenezer they founded on a high ridge, near the Savannah river called Red Bluff from the peculiar color of the soil. "Strobel's Salzburgers and their Descendants" has the following concerning the new town.

"On the east lay the Savannah with its "broad, smooth surface and its every va-"rying and beautiful scenery. On the "South was a stream, then called Little's

"Creek, but now known as Lackner's Creek
"and a large lake known as Neidlinger's
"Sea; while to the North, not very far
"from the town, was to be seen their old
"acquaintance, Ebenezer Creek, sluggish-
"ly winding its way to mingle with the wa-
"ters of the Savannah. The surrounding
"country was gently undulating, and cov-
"ered with a fine growth of forest trees,
"while the jessamine, the woodbine and
"the beautiful azalea with its variety of
"gaudy colors, added a peculiar richness to
the picturesque scene."

But unfortunately for the permanent
prosperity of the town, it was surrounded
by low swamps, which were subject to pe-
riodical inundation and consequently prej-
udicial to the health of the inhabitants. New Ebenezer within a short
time after its settlement gave manifest token of substantial growth and prosperity.
The houses were larger and more comfortable than those which had been built in the
old town. Gardens and farms were cleared,
inclosed and brought under creditable cultivation, and the sedate, religious inhabitants enjoyed the fruits of their industry.

Funds received from Germany for the purpose were employed in the erection of an
orphan house, in which for the lack of a
church, the community worshipped for several years.*   It is not necessary for the
purpose of this work to follow further the
history of New Ebenezer, except to say
that it became a town of considerable note
and the capital of Effingham County. The
people who lived there were exceedingly
religious, and for many years there was no
necessity for a Court of Justice. The children were brought up in the most decorous
ways, with a strictness hardly equalled by
New England in its most puritanic days,
and their early life was given to industry.
A large church was built there, and quite
a library was collected, but for all this prosperity, New Ebenezer, like the old, has
been numbered among the "Dead Towns
of Georgia." Jerusalem Church, a substantial brick structure there, still remains as
a monument of holy memories, but
all else of that smiling settlement has
passed away; it is Goldsmith's "Deserted
Village" over again:—

*History of Georgia.

"The sports are fled, and all the charms withdrawn;
Amidst thy bowers thy tyrant's hand is seen,
And desolation saddens all thy green:
One only master grasps the whole domain,
And half a tillage stints thy smiling plain;
No more thy glassy brook reflects the day,
But choak'd with sedges, works its winding way;
Along thy glades a solitary guest,
The hollow sounding bittern guards its nest;
Amidst the desert wilds the lapwing flies,
And tires their echoes with unvary'd cries.
Sunk are thy bowers in shapeless ruin all,
And the long grass o'er tops the mould'ring wall,
And, trembling, shrinking from the spoiler's hand
Far, far away thy children leave the land."

Why is it, in all nations, that so many towns, famous for being, as it were, the birthplaces of reforms, and of purer and better things, are permitted, by that Providence who rules the world, to become ruins or extinct?

CHAPTER II.

GIST, THE DUTCH PEDLER.

A Swa bia-Franconia Arrival—Birth of a Baby Boy
—A Pest to Ebenezer—The Unlicensed Pedler—
Wooes a Cherokee Maiden—Purchases Her for a
Wife—He Smokes and She Works—The Wigwam
—Indian Hospitality—Around the Dinner Kettle
—Sudden Disappearance—A Cause of American
"Blues."

These devout Salzburgers left in Bavaria another class far less religious in nature, who were a cross between the inhabitants of Ancient Swa bia and the
people of Ancient Franconia, who markedly retained some of the leading characteristics of the people from whom they
descended, viz., ignorance and superstition
on the one hand, and a wicked cunning on
the other. In the month of March, 1739,
when the worshippers had become fully established in their home in New Ebenezer,
they addressed a call through the Trustees
to their friends, relatives and countrymen

in the old country to come over and settle with them. Though they pledged the Trustees, that these friends should all be godly men, a family of Bavarians of the Swabia–Franconia Branch came over and with them took up their residence. They were influenced only by hope of gain, having no holy aspirations like those who came before them. Not long after their arrival, they had born to them a baby-boy, who was very markedly possessed of the leading traits of his Swabia–Franconia ancestors, which led him to grow up in ignorance, superstition and that cunning, which often, in after days, led him into doubtful enterprise. This Dutch boy named by his parents George Gist* grew up to be the bane of the village of New Ebenezer. He was too indolent to study and he would not work, and when he reached manhood, he could speak but a few words of English and of the Cherokee tongue he knew absolutely nothing. Though Ebenezer was still noted for its freedom from disreputable characters, George Gist chose to be among

*By some authorities Gisb.

that few. He could hardly be called a vaga-
bond as he possessed too much energy, but
he was held in so low repute that he could
not obtain a pedler's license, and he became a traveling trader of the contraband
order, trading and bartering without a license, and from the Indians often charging
a profit of two or three hundred per cent*.

*On Oct. 7th, 1763, King George prohibited all
provincial governors from granting lands, or issu-
ing land warrants, to be located upon any territory
lying west of the mountains, or west of those
streams which flow into the Atlantic, and all settlements by the subjects of Great Britain, west of the
sources of the Atlantic rivers. It was further decreed and required, "that all traders should
take a license from their respective governors for
carrying on commerce with the Indians." This proc-
lamation of the distant King was often disregarded,
and indeed it was impossible to prevent those inclined from trading more or less without the license
required by law.—*Ramsey*

An account is given in "The Annual Register of
1763, of the method one of these Indian traders took
to stir up trade among the Cherokees. It says: —

"Jeffreys, an Indian trader, having sold to the
Cherokees several garments of red baize. much of
the nature of the Highland uniform, for which he
had a valuable return of furs and deer-skins ; and his
excellency, the governor finding these things liked

One bright spring morning in 1768, this
George Gist, it is said, left Ebenezer. He
passed through Augusta, and taking the
path marked out by the Cherokees in
1740,* he entered the Cherokee Nation by

and the Cherokees not a little proud of their new
dress, ordered a very magnificent suit of rich scarlet, in the same form, and trimmed with silver tas-
sels, to be presented to each of their chiefs; so if
this humor holds, they might see the whole Cherokee nation clad in regimentals, which may probably
extend all over North America." On this subject
the editor of the "Register" reflected as follows: "As
a change in dress has been ever deemed, a step at
least, toward a change in manners, it would, perhaps, be well worth the while of our colonies to
supply all the savages in general, even gratis, with
garments of this kind. It would probably have one
good effect, if it had no other, that of rendering
them in time dependent upon us, by creating among
them a want, which neither themselves or any European nation, but the English, could supply."

*In this year there was a handsome fort at Au-
gusta, where there was a small garrison of twelve or
fifteen men besides officers. The safety the traders
derived from this fort drew them to that point. Another cause of the place, was the fertility of the land
around it. The Cherokees marked out a path from
Augusta to their nation, so that horsemen could
ride from Savannah to all parts of the Indian Nations.—*Annals of Tennessee.*

the northern mountains of Georgia. He
had two pack horses laden with merchan-
dise suited for Indian trade. In thus start-
ing out Gist was a violator of law. This he
well knew, for Capt. Stewart, the British
Superintendent of Indian affairs, was reg-
ulator of that traffic among them, and
none could lawfully engage in it without
license. But Gist chose to run any risk
there might be, and on this Spring morning in 1768 he started on a trading trip
among the Cherokees. On this round, he
saw a Cherokee maiden who pleased his
fancy. She in return was pleased with
him; a few glittering gewgaws from his
pack passed over to her father sealed the
marriage contract. Though her family
were not numbered among the chiefs of
the Cherokee tribes, they were prominent
and influential, and she had brothers* who
spoke in the Council. Even as George
Gist could not speak a word of Cherokee,

*One of these brothers was Ke-a-ha-ta-kee It is
stated that he was at one time President of Echota,
their ancient town of refuge. Like the Jews, the
Early Cherokees had a "City of Refuge" to which
an Indian having committed murder in his tribe
could fly for safety.

neither could she speak a word of Dutch
or English. At this early day, even, it was
no unusual thing for the Whites to make
these marriages with Cherokee girls. It
was a matter of convenience, for the early
Cherokee women were willing slaves, and
in all respects she was the typical Cherokee
woman of one hundred and twenty-five
years ago. In her early life, before this
marriage, she helped her mother about
the wigwam as much, if not more, than
the American girl of to-day helps hers.—
She cooked, she mended, dressed the venison and made ornamental work, and
though she was not accounted a handsome
maid, Gist seemed to appreciate her worth
and purchased her as his wife; and this
woman, as history records it, so long as
he lived with her, was a model Indian wife,
for she prided herself in permitting her
husband to do just nothing at all, and on
her success in this particular she based
her hope of heaven.

While our Dutch pedler smoked his
home-made pipe around the fire or joined
in the chase when his indolence would

allow, she cultivated the maize, even
cleared a piece of land for tillage; she
helped put up a wigwam; she prepared
and dried the skins, and fashioned them
into clothing, and cooked his food over
the wigwam fire. She even butchered the
game, saddled the horses, and cared for
them on his return; she brought the wood,
fetched the water,—and yet, though prac-
tically a slave, as she knew no better way,
she was accounted a very happy woman.
Her hope of happiness was based on her
devotion to her husband; so the more she
did for him, the more contented she became. Her home was the dream of Mogg
Megone over again, where:—

> "The Sum of Indian happiness!—
> A wigwam, where the warm sunshine
> Looks in among the groves of pine—
> A stream, where round thy light canoe,
> The trout and salmon dart in view,
> And the fair girl—   *   *   *
>   *   * plying in the dews of morn,
> Her hoe amidst the patch of corn,
> Or offering up at eve to thee,
> Thy birchen dish of hominy."

In short, all the duties of every kind re-
lating to the home, the family and its sur-

roundings devolved upon the Cherokee woman. It was her duty to relieve her husband of every drudgery and care; it was the business of the man to hunt and fish in time of peace, and fight for the protection of his wife and children in case of war, and it was not until 1826, that the Cherokees began to feel that the raising of corn and the management of their little plantations belonged exclusively to the male sex, and from that time, this so called barbarous nation strove to elevate woman to her appointed place, while in the States, the land of boasted civilization and enlightenment where missions have their spring and support, and contribution boxes are so freely passed for funds

Says Irving: "The Indian women were far from complaining of their lot. On the contrary, they despised their husbands could they stoop to any menial office, and would think it conveyed an imputation on their own conduct. It was the worst insult one virago could cast upon another in a moment of altercation. 'Infamous woman,' she would cry, 'I have seen your husband carrying wood into his lodge to make the fire. Where was his squaw that he should be obliged to make a woman of himself."

to convert far-off heathen, too many persist in apeing the laziness and custom of
those red barbarians of old, and become
store and street corner loafers, and pat-
rons of drinking saloons, while their tired
wives earn their bread by taking in sale
work.

But Gist soon wearied of Indian life
and the neat wigwam made largely by
his wife's own hands lost its attraction,
and one night, suddenly gathering together his effects he went away ; he never
returned, nor is there any record that he
was ever heard of more. And thus the
Cherokee wife was left alone in the wigwam, which, by the way, was not the
worst place to be left in after all ; for it
was warm and comfortable,* circular in
form, thirty or forty feet in diameter, constructed of forked pieces of timber, six
feet in length, placed in the ground, at
small distances from each other, in ver-
tical position supported by others placed
obliquely. Four taller beams placed in

*Millot.

the middle served as a support to the poles or rafters, which were covered with fine willow branches thickly matted with grass or clay. The door or entrance was four feet wide, a hole in the middle of the roof served as an escape for smoke and the admission of light. The beds and seats were made of the skins of different animals, but what is most important to us now, was a platform raised three feet from the floor and covered with the hairy skin of a bear. This was the reception seat for guests. At any hour of the day guests were welcome. No race is more hospitable to strangers if it be in time of peace than the Indian, and it is to be regretted, that the old fashioned hospitality of our New England people, followed so closely in the moccasin footprints of our Indians toward the setting sun. This hos-

*In the narrative of Col. James Smith, who was for many years a captive among the Indians. he gives an incident illustrative of Indian hospitality: "Tontileango went out to hunt, and when he was gone a Wyandotte came to our camp. I gave him a shoulder of venison which I had by the fire, well

pitality is characteristic with all Indians.

While George Gist remained in the wigwam, Indian hospitality was fully carried out. The savory smells, which escaped from the aperture at the top, drew many from other wigwams, who were made very welcome ; when the cooking was done, they would gather around a great earthen kettle, from which, having no knives or forks, with the most primative, but effective tools, their fingers, they would pick out the meat ; having only one meal per day, and that well and

roasted, and he received it gladly, told me he was hungry. and thanked me for my kindness. When Tontileango came home I told him that a Wyandotte had been to camp, and that I gave him a shoulder of venison. He told me that was very well, and I suppose you gave him also sugar and bears oil to eat with his venison. I told him I did not, as the sugar and bears oil were down in the canoe, I did not go for it. He replied, "You have acted just like a Dutchman. Do you not know, that when strangers come to our camp, we ought always give them the best we have?" I acknowledged that I was wrong. He said that he could excuse this, as I was but young, but I must learn to behave like a warrior and do great things, and never be found in such little actions.

thoroughly cooked, dyspepsia, that enemy to the white men and women of to-day
never dared approach the early Cherokee
people, and so this world, which God
made to look so charming and bright to
all humanity, never appeared to be a
gloomy place to them, as they never permitted a disordered stomach to blight
their hope of an eternity of bliss in their
"happy hunting ground" beyond.

CHAPTER III.

BIRTH OF SE-QUO-YAH.

Cotemporary History—Primitive Child-birth—The
Guest Reception Seat Occupied—Visit of the Old
Grand Parent—The Name—Cradle—An Indian
Lesson—True Elements of success—The Religion
of the Early Cherokee.

It was in the year 1770, when the people of New York erected the first pole, where the City Hall now stands, in favor of "Liberty," and all America was struggling to shake off the British yoke, that the real hero of our sketch was born. But George Gist had cared not to wait even for that event. Some time before the advent of the child, the deserted wife, according to the early custom of her tribe, alone and unattended, left her friends and kindred, and in a secluded thicket, far away from camp, she gave birth to her child, and thus the first music, that greeted this Indian child, was the sighing of the forest, the musical rustle of leaves and the song of Nature, which he loved through life, which seems to have been the inspiration of his genius and the key to his grand achievement. While the Dutch father was perhaps making new conquests in other localities, the deserted mother came back to her now lonely wigwam and placed on the guest's reception seat a cradle in which was her new-born child. And the father of this deserted Cherokee wife came in and

*The burdens of maternity to these simple children of the forest, strengthened by toil and inured to hardship, were generally light. According to the quaint account: "In one quarter of an hour a woman would be merry in the wigwam, and delivered and merry again: and in two days abroad, and after four or five days at work." In case of a difficult travail, the stern will and resolute fortitude of Indian character triumphed over nature, and scarcely a complaint was uttered, lest she should be esteemed worthy to be the mother only of cowards.

looked at his grandchild and seeing that
it was a boy, he gave a grunt of approval.
Had it been a girl, he would have turned
silently away to the wigwam fire, to count
by anticipation, the bright jewels or horses
she would bring, when she became of mar-
riageable age. As the Cherokee mother
stood by the guest reception seat, and
looked lovingly on her sleeping child, her
mind turned in silent sadness toward her
truant husband, to whom she had been,
and to whose memory she was ever after
true; then and there, she named her child
Se-quo-yah, which in the musical language
of his people means "he guessed it."*

*Authorities differ concerning the naming of Se-
quo-yah. Rev. C. C. Torrey, for many years a
missionary among the Cherokees, in a personal letter writes us that it was not given until after the
invention of the alphabet, and had reference to
guessing it out; but W. A. Phillips, who prepared
an extended account of Se-quo-yah for Harper's
Magazine, and who was acquainted with the family,
and even had one of Se-quo-yah's sons in his regi-
ment during the civil war says: "The deserted
mother called her *babe* Se-quo-yah; his fellow
clansmen, *as he grew up*, gave him an English
name, that of his father, or something like it," and

The cradle in which Se-quo-yah slept,
was like those all Indians used. A piece
of dried buffalo hide cut in proper shape,
then turned on itself, and fastened together with strings; the face always exposed,
the whole then tightly fastened to a board
to which were attached straps, which
passed over the head, so the mother could
carry the child on her back as she journied, or to the field where she worked, for
hang it on an alder bush near by. In a
cradle like this, Se-quo-yah staid for ten
months. Think of it! For ten long months
except to be bathed once a day, did Se-
quo-yah stay strapped in his hard cradle,
which was either hung on a tree branch,
or packed away at an angle of forty-five degrees in some out of the way corner of
the wigwam. Doubtless the reader will
think that there must have been a very
squally time of it if little Se-quo-yah was
brought up in this way. But it was not so.

in English he is usually spoken of as George Guess.
Se-quo-yah is still the name the Cherokees fondly
cling to. One of the counties of their nation bears
his name, and one of their literary institutions is
called after him.

Indian children of those days were educated not to fuss. What a difference between the teaching of this Indian and some of our white mothers! The first lesson the Indian mother taught her children was that of self dependence and obedience. The Good Lord gave to this simple Indian woman, Se-quo-yah's mother, an intuition that half her child's squalls were not from the stomach's ache, but from the evil suggestions of Satan himself; so having given him due care, she placed Se-quo-yah in the most out of the way corner of the wigwam or hung him on an alder bush outside, and if Satan did prompt him to an unnecessary squall, she grasped Se-quo-yah's nose between her thumb and forefinger and held on until the little one was nearly suffocated; she then let go, only to seize and smother him again at his first attempt at an outbreak, and thus in the very first month of his life was Se–quo–yah taught that obedience was the best policy and unlike many white children, who are pampered in their early life to their future destruction, Se-quo-yah grew up strong,

selfreliant and obedient.* Let the life of
this barbarous mother teach us this lesson of judicious training—not her methods

"It is but justice," says a writer, after speaking of
these peculiar methods of rearing children, "to bear
our testimony to the maternal affection of the Indian
women, in which they fall nothing behind their
more civilized and more polished sisters. We have
often marked the anxiety of the Indian mother
bending over her sick child; her untiring watchful-
ness, and so far as a mother's love can make it so,
refined attentions to its claims upon her tenderness.
In times of danger, we have witnessed its anxiety
for security, and her fearless exposure of her own
person for its protection. We have looked npon the
rough-clad warrior in the solitude of his native
forest attired in the skins of beasts or wrapped about
with his blankets, and realized all our preconceived
impressions of his ferocity and savage-like appearance—but when we have entered the lodge and beheld in the untutored mother, and amid the rude
circumstances of her condition, the same parental
love for her children, that we have seen in other
lands, we almost forgot that we stood at the thresh-
old of the ruthless savage, whose pursuits and feelings we had supposed to have nothing in common
with ours, and have felt, that both as children of
one father, we were brothers of the same blood—
heirs of the same infirmities—victims of the same
passions, and though in different degrees, bound
down to the same common feelings of our nature."

but her principle and purpose. It is a
grave error of the American mother to do
too much for her children when they are
small and too long delay teaching them
the lesson of self reliance. Of all the elements of success in life none is more vital
than to be ones own helper, and not look
to others for support. It is the secret of
intellectual growth and vigor, the master
key that unlocks all difficuities in all pro-
fessions and every calling. In all her seem-
ing rudeness, Phillips tells us, "No truer
mother ever lived and cared for her child.
She reared him with the most watchful
tenderness. With her own hands she cleared her little field and cultivated it, and
carried her babe while she drove up the
cows and milked them." Se-quo-yah's
mother and her parents had no established
religion. They were not idolaters, for they
did not worship idols; yet like many Cherokees of that day, they were more religious than the average white man. In the
early days of the Cherokee people no warrior thought himself secure until he had
addressed his guardian angel, and no

hunter ever dreamed of success until before the rising sun* he had asked assistance of his God, to whom on his return
at eventide he forgot not to offer sacrifice.
And thus the early Indian, though having no established religion, believed in a
God and worshipped him, and this adoration of his good god was generally far
greater than a white man's love. We
are taught in childhood on our mother's
knee that certain things are right and

*Even the early Cherokees gave the East due rev-
erence in all their solemn ceremonials, especially
in the opening of the council. Says Irving, "All
being seated the old Seneschal prepared the pipe†
of ceremony or council, and having lit it handed it
to the chief. He inhaled the sacred smoke, gave a
puff upward to the heaven, then downward to the
earth, *then toward the East*; after this it was as
usual passed from mouth to mouth, each holding it
respectfully until his neighbor had taken several
whiffs, and now the grand council was considered
as opened in due form."

†Much labor was bestowed on the ornamentation
of these pipes both common and ceremonial. They
often represented birds and animals, but especially
did the Cherokees make their pipes in human
shape, as Adair remarks, not much to be com-
mended for their modesty.

others wrong. Morality is inculcated
with our religion, and we cannot divorce
them. But the religion that Se-quo-yah's
mother taught him, though crude and
undeveloped, became as firmly seated in
his belief as Christianity is in the faith
of the Christian, but it was a religion
with no moral code. It taught no duty or
obligation to God or man. Right and
wrong were abstract terms and had no
meaning to Se–quo-yah in his early life.
Hence he believed all right that he wished
to do and all wrong that opposed him. It
was right to steal horses from another
tribe or a white man,* but wrong to steal
from his own tribe. Beside the "good
god" to whom he bowed so reverently
toward the East, that he might be aided
in all of his undertakings, be protected

---

*The first known battle between the Whites and
Cherokees was the result of thus taking a few
horses. A few Cherokees took several horses from
the Whites, and they gave them no quarter. They
murdered several Cherokees, and the feud thus began was of long continuance. The Cherokees took
conciliatory measures, which the Whites rejected.

from danger and privations and to be
given all the good and pleasurable things
of life, Se-quo-yah's mother taught him
that toward the setting sun dwelt the
"bad god" the red man's enemy, and that
from him came all the privations, disas-
ters and life's misfortunes. And Se-quo-
yah grew up, believing that there was to
be for him a happy hunting ground, a
belief that answered the same purpose to
this untutored savage as St. John's vision
of the New Jerusalem does to us.*

Around the wigwam fire Se-quo-yah
was taught, that before the good Indian
dies, he orders his favorite horse to be
slain, that he may enjoy with him an
eternity of beautiful pastures; that he
would need him to hunt beyond the milky

*The idea of a future state was of very early or-
igin. A missionary of the A. B. C. F. M., in 1824,
had an interview with an aged chief whose boyhood
dated previous to the birth of Se-quo-yah. He said
that when he was young, he was told that they went
to another country when they died, where were very
many people, and great towns and villages, "but
we never talked much about those things."

way of the sky, which he believed to be
the wide road of the Indian dead,
made white by the myriads of journeying
ghosts; that he would need him, as he
hunted the phantom deer or buffalo, to get
phantom food, or phantom clothes for his
own phantom body. And Se-quo-yah's
mother taught him in the simple language
of her tribe, that in the region of the
hereafter he might expect phantom pain,
phantom hunger, and that all the ills that
flesh is heir to would follow him there
except death. She bade him take care
of his body here, for should he become
one legged on earth, he would be one
legged in the happy hunting ground beyond; if he lost an eye on earth, he would
continue to grope darkly through all time;
if he died in health, he would be a beautiful phantom, but if he died after a dis-
.tressing illness, he must forever be a decrepit spirit; if he died at night there
could be only an eternity of darkness;
in short a mutilated Indian body meant a
mutilated Indian soul. And Se-quo-yah

in boyhood believed that but two things
could keep his soul from the happy hunting ground ;—if he should be scalped his
soul was lost; if he should be strangled,
it never could escape. Such were the beliefs of the Cherokee people in the days
of Se-quo-yah's boyhood a century ago,
but naturally susceptible to new truths,
these beliefs changed from time to time,
and in 1817, when the American Board
established mission stations among them,
they declared that no other barbarous nation had been so willing to accept the Bible as this. Of his later religious belief
in his manhood Phillip's says :—

"Se-quo-yah, who never saw his father
and never could utter a word in the German tongue, still carried deep in his nature, an odd compound of Indian and
German trancendentalism ; essentially Indian in opinion, but German in instinct
and thought. He talked with his associ-
ates upon all the knotty points of law, religion and art. Indian Theism and Pan-
theism were measured against the gospel

as taught by the land-seeking, fur-buying adventurers. A good class of missionaries had indeed entered the Cherokee Nation ; but the shrewd Se-quo-yah and the disciples this stoic taught among the mountains, had just sense enough to weigh the good and the bad to-gether and to strike an impartial balance as the footing of this new proselyting race. It has been erroneously stated that Se–quo–yah was a believer in or practiced the old Indian religious rites. Christianity had, indeed, done little more for him than to unsettle the pagan idea, but it had done that."

Se-quo-yah seems to have never been on good terms with the missionaries, even though his alphabet was at last accepted by them, when they saw him—

"The Cadmus of the blind,
Giving the dumb lip language,
The idiot clay a mind."

yet it is only too evident that a few looked upon him as an interloper, who by his invention, had taken from them the laurels they strove to win.

CHAPTER IV.

FROM BOYHOOD TO MANHOOD.

Boyhood Pursuits—Important help to his Mother—
Silver-smith—Black-smith—Trade-mark—Sacred
Pipe—Debauch—Remorse—A Good Samaritan—
Reformation, and Good Work among his Peo-
ple.

The days of the Revolution were the
days of Se-quo-yah's boyhood. His mother was a woman of uncommon energy, and
Se-quo-yah being of a different temper
than other Indian boys of his time, and
many Yankee boys of our time, felt it no
disgrace to labor and to help her. Says
Phillips:—"He lived alone with his mother
and had no old man to teach him the use
of the bow. He would wander alone in
the forest and showed early mechanical

genius in carving with his knife many objects from pieces of wood. He employed his boyish leisure in building houses in the forest. As he grew older, these mechanical pursuits took a more useful shape. He first exercised his genius in making an improved kind of wooden milkpans and skimmers for his mother. Then he built her a milk-house, with all suitable conveniences, on one of those grand springs that gurgle from the mountains of the old Cherokee Nation. As a climax, he even helped her to milk her cows, and he also cleared additions to her fields and worked on them with her." Another account says: "Se-quo-yah's mother maintained herself by her own exertions. That she was a woman of some capacity is evident from the undeviating affection for herself with which she inspired her son, and the influence she exercised over him. Her property consisted chiefly in horses and cattle, that roamed in the woods, and of which she owned a considerable number. Her farm consisted of eight acres. He took care of the cattle and horses, and when he grew to sufficient size, would break the colts to saddle and harness." To his mother, without doubt, was due all the energy and perseverance of his nature; his meditative and philosophical inclinations came from his father or dated beyond him, and at last developed into an odd compound of Indian and German trancendentalism. But one trait he seemed to inherit from his father direct, and that was his love of trade and barter. Indeed, he also became a travelling trader, though not a contraband like his father. The Cherokee woman married or single owned her property in her own right, and in time Se-quo-yah's mother had contrived to get a stock of goods and she traded with her countrymen. She taught Se-quo-yah to be a good judge of furs and he would go on expeditions with hunters, and would select such skins as he wanted for his mother before they returned. Often he came back heavily laden with peltries, which his mother exchanged for articles of European make. A hatchet, a pocket looking-glass, a piece of scarlet cloth, paints, guns, and powder were exchanged for furs. The exchange was necessarily slow, but the profits realized were large. In the valleys of the Ohio and the Tennessee, the English and French still hunted the buffalo, and Sequo-yah often paid visits to these hunters with pack-horse trains for his mother. When his mother died he still occupied her cabin which soon became the resort of all his lively countrymen, for he was the genial story teller of his tribe. As he grew toward manhood, his mechanical ingenuity rapidly developed. For his goods he now received the broad silver pieces of the Spaniards, and the old French and English coins. This silver he beat into rings and broad, ornamented silver bands for the head. He made some handsome breastplates and necklaces of his own invention, also bells for the ankles and rings for the toes. He soon became the greatest silver-smith of his tribe, as his articles excelled all similar manufactures among his countrymen.

From the earliest days, the Southern

Indians had been marked for their works of skill. Famous were the arrow-makers of this region—

> "Making arrow-heads of jasper,
> Arrow-heads of chalcedony."

"These arrow and spear points were remarkable for beauty of material and excellency of workmanship. Party-colored jaspers, smoky, milky and sweet-water quartz, pure crystals, chalcedony and varieties of flint and chert were the favorite stones from which these implements were fashioned."* From marine, fluviatile, and lacustrine shells were manufactured pendants, beads, arm-guards, masks, pins, drinking-cups, spoons and money. The imposing calumet, with its long stem adorned with feathers was often made of serpentine, gneiss, steatite oolite, soapstone and a tough stone composed of mica and a dark brown feldspar.

Observation appears to have been a keynote in Se-quo-yah's progressive career. He was always foremost in what

*History of Georgia.

ever he undertook, and as we have said
was the best silver-smith of his tribe, but
he was never taught the trade. In later
years, after the white men had thickly
settled his nation, he resolved to be a
blacksmith. He never asked to be taught,
but visiting their shops, he freely used
his eyes, and with them learned how to
use his hands. Phillips remarks:—
"When he bought the necessary material and went to work it is characteristic
that his first performance was to make
his bellows and his tools, and those who
afterward saw them say that they were
well made." Among the leading chiefs
in the days of Se-quo-yah's young manhood were Crawling Snake, Path-killer,
Big Half Breed, Gentleman Town, Big
Cabin, Major Riley, Rising Fawn and
Charles Hicks. The latter had picked up
a little learning at the Moravian school*

*In 1733, the Trustees of Georgia offered Count
Zinzendorf a tract of land to be colonized by the
Brethren; this offer was gladly accepted, in the
hope that a way might thus be opened for preaching

was interested in religious matters, and
had more than a passing interest in Se-quo-
yah.   One day while working at his trade
of silver-smith, the idea of a trademark
dawned upon his mind, and he went to
his friend Hicks and asked him to write his
English name. What followed is thus related by Phillips:—"The real name of his
father was George Gist. It is now written
by the family as it has long been called in
the tribe when his English name is used—
"Guest." Hicks, remembering a word
that sounded like it wrote George Guess.
It was a "rough guess," but answered the
purpose. The silversmith was as ignorant of English as he was of any written
language. Being a fine workman, he made
in his Blacksmith shop a steel die, a fac-
simile of the name written by Hicks, and
with this he put his "trade mark" on his
silver wares and it is borne, to this day,
on many of these ancient works of art
in the Cherokee Nation".

the gospel to the Creeks Chickasaw and Cherokee
Indians.   Moravian Schools were organized the following year.

Thus for years, Se-quo-yah, when not engaged in the chase, of which he was passionately fond, traded in furs, made Indian jewels and forged in his little shop and was accounted quite well-to-do by his tribe.

Through life he was an inveterate user of tobacco, and for this he certainly is not to be accorded blame for the pipe was ever esteemed by the Cherokee as a sacred object, and tobacco a divine gift. With them, smoking at times became a devotional exercise, as they believed the incense of tobacco was pleasing to the "Father of Life." The ascending smoke was selected as the most suitable medium for communicating with the great unknown. Says Longfellow :—

"Gitche Manito, the mighty,
The Great Spirit, the Creator,
Smiled upon his helpless children !
And in silence all the warriors
Broke the red stone of the quarry,
Smoothed and formed it into Peace-Pipes,
Broke the long reeds by the river,
Decked them with their brightest feathers,

And departed each one homeward,
While the Master of Life, ascending,
Through the opening of cloud-curtains,
Through the doorways of the heaven,
Vanished from before their faces.
In the smoke that rolled around him,
The Pukwana of the Peace-Pipe."

We now come to a page in Se-quo-yah's history that gladly would we leave out. Civilized white man taught this barbarous Indian to indulge in the intoxicating cup. A vicious hospitality surrounded him, which led him onward in his course until, at the age of thirty-five he found his business seriously impaired and himself degenerated into almost a common sot. Says Phillips on this subject: —

"With the acuteness that comes of this foreign stock he learned to buy his liquor by the keg. This species of economy is as dangerous to the red as to the white race. The auditors who flocked to hear him were not likely to diminish, while the philosopher furnished both dogmas and the whiskey. Long and deep debauches were often the consequence.

Still it was not in his nature to be a wild shouting drunkard ; when he was too far gone to play the mild sedate philosopher, he began that monotonous singing whose melody carried him back to the days when the shadow of the whiteman never darkened the forest, and the Indian canoe alone rippled the tranquil waters. Then ashamed he would wander away to the woods, and sleep off the effect of his debauch, and he never returned among his people again without being thoroughly ashamed." A little over three miles from his cabin lived Col. Lowrey, a Cherokee noted for many good works among his people. He was deeply interested in Sequo-yah and his genius. He regretted to see his downward course, and he expostulated often with him, until he saw the reasonableness of his warning and with an almost superhuman effort,—

"One brave and manful struggle,—
He gained the solid land."

he gave up his drink, and ever after he was enrolled for temperance. Think of it !

A barbarian sot saying "I will" and becoming a temperance man, while around
us are hundreds and thousands of bum-
mers, wearing the garb of civilization,
who are saying "I can't" and with this as
their watchword going down to drunk-
ards' graves. When Col. Lowrey in
connection with David Brown drew up a
temperance pledge, many Cherokees
through Sequoyah's influence signed the
pledge—and kept it too.

Says Colton's North American Indians :
he continued to employ himself in black-
smithing for some years, and in the meanwhile turned his attention to the art of
drawing. He made many sketches of
horses, cattle, deer, houses and other familiar objects, which were as rude as
those which the Indians draw upon their
dressed skins, but which improved so
rapidly as to present at length, a very tol-
erable resemblance of the figures intended to be copied. He had probably at this
time never seen a picture or an engrav-
ing, but was led to these exercises by

the stirring of an innate propensity for the imitative arts. He became extremely popular. Amiable, accommodating, and unassuming, he displayed an industry uncommon among his people, and a genius which elevated him in their eyes as a prodigy. They flocked to him from the neighborhood, and from distant settlements, to witness his skill and to give him employment; and the untaught Indian gazed with astonishment at one of his own race, who had spontaneously caught the spirit, and was rivaling the ingenuity of civilized man.

CHAPTER V.

FESTIVALS, GAMES AND DANCES.

Ball-playing—Conjurers—The Magic Seven—Conjuring for Health—The Health Roast—Tradition Keeping—Green Corn Dance—Chungke—A War Song.

Se-quo-yah was the leader in many of the Indian sports; the chase was to him a passionate delight; as a fisherman none could him excell; of all athletic games he was the life, his favorite being the Indian game of ball. A description of one of these early games of ball as played by the early Cherokees is described as follows by an eye witness:—

*The grounds were a beautiful hickory level entirely in a state of nature, upon

*History of Walton County, Ga.

which had been erected several tents containing numerous articles, mostly of Indian manufacture, which were the stakes to be won or lost in the contest. The two contending parties were composed of fifty men each, mostly in a state of nudity, and having their faces painted in a fantastical manner and were headed by their chiefs. The war whoop was then sounded by one party and then by the other, and was continued alternately, as they advanced slowly and in regular order toward each other toward the center of the ground allotted for the contest. Two parallel lines of stakes are driven into the ground near each other, each extending for about one hundred yards, and having the space of one hundred yards between them. In the center of these lines were the contending towns, headed by their chiefs, each having in their hands two wooden spoons, curiously carved, not unlike our large iron spoons. The object of these spoons is to throw up the ball. The ball was made of deerskin wound around a piece of spunk.

To carry the ball through one of the lines mentioned above is the purpose to be accomplished. Every time the ball is carried through the line counts one. The game is commenced by one of the chiefs throwing up the ball to a great height by means of the wooden spoons. As soon as the ball was thrown up, the contending parties mingled together. If the chief of the opposite party catches the ball as it descends with his spoons, which he exerts his utmost skill to do, it counts one for his side. The respective parties stand prepared to catch the ball if there should be a failure on the part of their chiefs to do so. The strife begins. The chief has failed to catch the ball. A stout warrior has caught it, and endeavors with all speed to carry it to his lines, when a faster runner knocks his feet from under him, wrests the ball from him, and triumphantly makes his way with the prize to his own line; but when he almost reaches the goal, he is overtaken by one or more of his opponents, who endeavor to take it from him. The struggle becomes general, and it is often the case that serious personal injuries are inflicted. It is very common during the contest to let the ball fall to the ground. The strife now ceases for a time, until the chiefs again array their bands. The ball is again thrown up, and the game continued as above described. Sometimes half an hour elapses before either side succeeds in making one in the game. It was usual at these ball-plays for each party to have their conjurers at work at the time the game was going on; their stations were near the center of each line. In their hands were shells, bones of snakes

There was a tradition among the Indians that the line between the Creeks and the Cherokees commenced on the Chattahoochee, about the Lower Shallow Ford, running out to the ridge dividing the Etowah and the Chattahoochee rivers, around to the head waters of the Tallapoosa and those streams that flow into the Etowah, and thence on to the Coosa River. At a ball play in which the Cherokees and Creeks were engaged, the latter staked that portion of their territory that lay south ot this line, and the former won the game and obtained possession of the territory, in which the counties of Cobb, Paulding and Polk are now included.—*Historical Collections of Georgia.*

and other articles of conjury. These conjurers often came great distances. They were estimated according to their ages, and it was supposed that by their charms they could influence the game.

These conjurers* played an important part and were especially consulted in the case of serious illness. Seven has ever been a mystic number among barbarous and semi-barbarous tribes. It was the mystic symbol in the days of the Jews, and even among us to-day are those who have the greatest faith in the seventh son. In case of sickness among the Cherokees, a conjurer was called in, when he immediately dispatched seven of the best hunters with orders to kill seven deer, and to carry them to an appointed place. The conjurer then fasted in the woods, and collected herbs of medicinal qualities, or those supposed to have important powers with evil spirits. While the people were assembling he crumpled the magical herbs in an earthen pot, hanging over the fire, in which he had previously placed the meat in a lib-

*Missionary Herald.

eral supply of water. In the meanwhile,
the conjurer kept tasting the compound,
which he shared with the braves around
him. Then he commanded all the women old and young, to dance seven times
around the fire, drumming on kegs. One
after another, the men and boys join in the
dance until the hour of sunrise, when all
again partake of the nauseous compound.
Seven men are then chosen to stay and
watch the pot and keep it filled with fresh
herbs till the days when the conjurer's
spell is over, and the guests depart bearing
with them a portion of the magic compound, in which to wash and in seven days
to return for the final ceremonies. Then
the conjurer takes his fees, which are the
skins of deer and strings of pure white
beads from every person present, for thus
he would keep them from disease. But for
all this disease would come, and often, in
those early days, when one fell sick, the
conjurer would cause to be hollowed in the
ground a hole, over which he ordered to
be built a wigwam, constructed of soil
and stone. Around this he would build

a furious fire until the wigwam smoked
with fervent heat, until the close interior
had reached almost an oven temperature.
Then the Indian doctor having raked away
the fires, into the interior of this smoking
wigwam would thrust his patients, leaving
them until they roasted or perspired. Then
from this oven the conjurer would pull
out the perspiring and often dying patient,
and plunge him in the river where the
water flowed coldest, and then repeat the
treatment from time to time, until the
conjurer grew tired or the patient died.*

*The "Morning Star" of Dec. 1884 has the follow-
ing, the tribe not named :—

"The women make a kind of hut, of bended wil-
lows, which is nearly circular, and if for one or two
persons only, not more than fifteen feet in circum-
ference, and three or four in height. Over these
they lay the skins of the buffalo, &c. and in the
center of the hut, they place heated stones. The
Indian then enters, perfectly naked, with a dish of
water in his hand, a little of which he occasionally
throws on the hot stones, to create steam, which, in
connection with the heat, puts him into a profuse
perspiration. In this situation he will remain for
about an hour; but a person unaccustomed to endure such heat, could not sustain it for half that
time. They sweat themselves in this manner, they

In the early days of the Cherokee people, important incidents were communica-
ted, and their remembrance preserved by
wampum, formed of strings of beads, orig-
inally made of white clay, in a rude manner, by themselves, so arranged as to bear
a distinct resemblance to the objects intended to be delineated. The belts were particularly devoted to the preservation of
speeches, the proceedings of councils, and
the formation of treaties. They had an officer, whose duty it was from time to time
to repeat the speeches and narratives connected with those belts to impress them
fully upon his memory and transmit them
to his successor. At a certain time each
year they were taken from their places of
deposit, and exposed to the whole tribe,
while the history of each was publicly recited. Could a collection of these ancient

say, in order that their limbs may become more
supple, and they more alert in pursuing animals
which they are desirous of killing. They also consider sweating a powerful remedy for the most of
diseases. As they come from sweating, they frequently plunge into a river, or rub themselves
with snow."

belts be made to day, and the accompany-
ing narratives recorded, it would afford
curious and interesting materials, reflect-
ing, no doubt, much light upon the former situation and history of the Indians.
In later years the beads were discon-
tinued, but still the traditions were handed down by some old man appointed for
the purpose. In each assembly of the
Cherokees, he was expected to rehearse
the story of their early history and sub-
sequent achievements. This he did in a
set speech, continuing his discourse al-
though the company might be dancing,
or however inattentive. Many of those
traditions were early forgotten. In the
mutation and migrations of the various
tribes, misfortunes pressed heavily upon
them; the old men died and with them
the memories of a lifetime.

The Green Corn Dance was the annual festival, the origin of which is not
now known. At this the conjurer prepared a sort of medicine, on a day appointed by the old people, and seven fam-

ilies were appointed to furnish corn foɪ
the feast. Every one was obliged to take
a portion of the medicine, and a portion
was offered, by throwing corn into the
fire before any one could eat. Before the
feast it was unlawful to eat of the new
corn of the season, and no person was
ever known to transgress. After that all
might eat freely.

"Chungke* was the great gambling
game among the early Cherokees, in
which the contestant engaged from morning until night, caring nothing for the
sun's rays, staking their ornaments, apparel, weapons, and even wife's personal
liberty upon the hazard, and refraining
not from its excitement, until all was lost
or utter prostration forbade further exer-
tion. The spaces prepared for playing
this game have not fully disappeared in
the old Cherokee country, Rectangular
in outline, slightly elevated, rendered
level, and freed from all impediments
such as roots and stones, their surface

*History of Georgia, by C. C. Jones.

was some times hardened by a flooring
of rammed clay. Were we called upon
to suggest a class of articles, which am-
ply expressed the patient industry and
mechanical skill of these primitive work-
ers in stone we would be inclined to select those beautiful objects known as the
discoidal stones with which this game
was played. They were made of furrugi-
nous quartz, marble, agate, and a hard,
black, close-grained stone. Polished to
the last degree, they were fashioned with
a mathematical accuracy, which could not
be excelled were the skill of a modern
workman with compass and metalic tools
invoked. Little now remains save these
stones to remind us of the former existence and prevalence of this popular game
characterized by severe exercise, singular dexterity and desperate ventures".

The dances* of the Indians were not
designed to be graceful amusements, nor
healthful exercises, and bore no resemblance to the elegant, joyous scenes of

*Colton's North American Indians.

the ball room. The music, the lights, the
women, and above all the charms thrown
about the hilarious exhibition, by cour-
tesy and gallantry of the parties—all of
these were wanting in the war dance, in
which the warriors only engaged. It was
a ceremony, not a recreation, and conducted with the seriousness belonging to
an important duty. The mnsic was a monotonous beating upon a rude drum with
no melody or tune. As they passed in a
circle, they uttered low, dismal and syllabic sounds, which they repeated with
but perceptible variations, throughout the
exhibition. The songs were in fact short
disjointed sentences, alluding to some
victory, passion for revenge, the object
of which was to keep alive the recollec-
tion of injury, and to excite the tribe
against its enemies. Mr. Johnson, who
spent many years among the Indians and
was familiar with their language, many
years ago gave to Thomas L. McKinney,
who was then the U. S. Secretary of War,
the following translation of a war song :–

On that day when our heroes lay low, lay low,
  On that day when our heroes lay low;
I fought by their side, and thought ere I died,
  Just vengeance to take of the foe, the foe,
  Just vengeance to take of the foe.

On that day when our Chieftains lay dead, lay
    dead,
  On that day when our Chieftains lay dead;
I fought hand to hand, at the head of my band,
  And here on my breast have I bled, have I bled,
  And here on my breast have I bled.

Our Chiefs shall return no more, no more,
  Our Chiefs shall return no more;
And their brothers in war, who can't show scar
    for scar,
  Like women their fates shall deplore, deplore,
  Like women their fates shall deplore.

Five winters in hunting we'll spend, we'll spend,
  Five winters in hunting we'll spend;
Then our youth grown to men, to the war lead
    again,
  And onr days like our fathers, we'll end, we'll
    end,
  And our days like our fathers we'll end.

CHAPTER VI.

A WARRIOR'S CONQUEST.

Warrior Making—War-dance and Song—Would make him Dreadful—Fair Honors sought by the Cherokees—Sequoyah's Courtship—Marriage— The Early Cherokee Woman—Nature's Teaching —He Dreams and She Works—A Family Disagreement Consequent.

Among the very many entertaining accounts of early Indian customs, none are more novel than those of warrior making and the preparations for war. No two tribes appear to have had the same customs, and even different branches of the same tribe had their peculiar practices. The redmen of the Ohio Valley* at their war dance had both vocal and instrumen-

*Narrative of Col. James Smith.

tal music, they had a short hollow drum, closed at one end with water in it, and parchment stretched over the open end thereof, which they beat with one stick, and made a sound nearly like a muffled drum. All those who were going on this expedition, collected together and formed and an old Indian then began to sing, and timed the music by beating on this drum as the ancients formerly timed their music by beating the tabor. On this the warriors began the advance, or moved forward in concert, as well disciplined troops would march with fife and drum. Each warrior had a tomahawk, spear, or war mallet in his hand, and they all moved regularly toward the east and thensuddenly wheeling quick about and with a hideous yell, they would move quickly back again. Then came the war song ; in performing this only one sung at a time, in bending posture, with a tomahawk in his hand, while all the other warriors were engaged in calling aloud a watch-word, which was con-

stantly repeated while the war-song was
going on; when the warrior that was
singing had ended his song, he struck the
war post with his tomahawk, and with a
loud voice told what warlike exploits he
had done, and what he now intended
to do, which were answered by the other
warriors with loud shouts of applause.

Some who had not intended to go to
war before would become so much animated by this performance, that they took
the tomahawk and sung the war-song,
which was answered with shouts of joy;
they were then initiated into the present
marching company. Another method of
warrior-making is told by McKinney.
The usage of the nation, made it requisite
that martial training should be preceded
by a formal dedication to the life of a
warrior, and invocation to the Great Spirit
to endue him with courage and good fortune. For this purpose, the parents so-
licited the assistance of a warrior, whose
numerous achievements in battle had established for him a high reputation, and

whose sagacity and valor gave him, in the
estimation of his tribe, the envied rank of
an Ulysses.   The assent of the war-chief
was conveyed in the brief avowal, that
he "would make him dreadful." The
ceremony took place immediately.   The
hoary brave standing upon the brink of a
mountain stream called upon the Great
Spirit to fill the mind of the young warrior
with warlike inclinations and his heart
with courage   He then with the bone of
a wolf, the end of which terminated in
several sharp points, scratched the naked boy, from the palm of the hand and
along the front of the arm across the
breast and along the other arm to the
hand, and in like manner lines were
drawn from the heels upward to the
shoulders, and from the shoulders over
the breast down to the feet, and from
the back of one hand along the back and
to the back of the other hand. The lines
thus made each covered a space of two
inches in width, and consisted of parallel
incissions, which penetrated through the

skin, and caused an effusion of blood along the entire extent. He was then required to plunge into the stream and bathe, after which the war chief washed his whole body with a decoction of medicinal herbs, and in conclusion he was commanded not to associate with the female children or to sit near a woman, nor in short, to suffer one to touch him for a period of seven days. At the end of this time the war-chief came to him, and after delivering an address to the Great Spirit, placed before the young candidate food consisting of partridges and mush. The partridge was used on this occasion because, in its flight, this bird makes a noise with its wings resembling thunder, while in sitting or walking, it is remarkably silent and difficult to discover —and thus were indicated the clamor of contest, and the cautious stealth which should govern the movements of the warrior at all other times.

The above is taken from the story and life of Major Ridge, a distinguished Cherokee.

The Cherokees won their honors fairly;
their rank as warriors was not obtained on
the impulse of a momentary excitement.
So far as we are able to determine, there
are no records to show how Se-quo-yah
became a warrior. It was doubtless from
his skill and bravery in the chase; it was
not through thirst for human blood. It is
said to have been the custom of the early
Cherokee chiefs, at the age of sixteen, to
send the young Indians to the woods,
where, before their return home, they were
expected to do some daring deed. In imagination now, we must follow these
young braves, taught as they were to
glory in the chase and to rejoice in blood.
Before us passes a vision where they per-
form many cruel and warlike deeds, engage in a struggle with warriors of hostile
tribes, or in fierce conflict with panther
or bear. Now the vision changes; homeward, besmeared with blood and often
wounded, the party of young braves pur-
sue their way and are welcomed by older
chiefs and heroes of many battles. Then
all assemble at the Council Lodge, where

the brave old chiefs, with utmost gravity listen to the story of the young braves' deeds. Each in his turn still frenzied with excitement, in bounds, in yells and frantic gesture, pour forth in almost incoherent language, a recital of special deeds on which he based his claims. The chiefs deliberate and if the young braves' acts seem of sufficient valor, the chiefs proclaim them "Warriors" from the door of Council Lodge. In some such way as this Se-quo-yah was proclaimed a warrior, and then his first conquest was to get a wife according to the custom of that time. Having selected the Indian maid of his fancy, he painted himself in the highest style of Indian art, the blending to-gether of nearly every color of the rainbow. He greased his hair, smoothed out his locks and adorned them with Indian jewels and enveloping himself in a buffalo hide, he repaired to the lodge of his chosen one. Hours he stood there by the wigwam door, ever smiling, never speaking, and day by day he kept up these silent visits until the old Indians fixed a price on the girl.

The price fixed, the Indian girl gave the first demure smile of encouragement. Up to this time neither had spoken a word to the other in private. Then Se-quo-yah hastened home to obtain the horses and robes, which were to be the price of his bride. He tied the horses near her wigwam door, and went home in doubt and fear to pass the night. Even before the sun arose next morning he hastened to the wigwam of his love, and joyfully he found the horses stabled, and that she had neatly packed away the robes. It was thus he knew his suit was not rejected. No other ceremony of marriage was performed, the price was paid, the gifts accepted and the girl was Se-quo-yah's wife. This wife which Se-quo-yah took was no common Indian maiden. In form she was like the women of her race; she was tall, erect, and of a delicate frame; her features formed with perfect symmetry, and her countenance was cheerful and amiable. Both in her soul and that of Se-quo-yah was a higher intuition than appeared to be bestowed on any other of the Chero-

kee tribe. For a time their sympathies
were one, and for a time their lives
were markedly happy. For all nature
spoke in plainest utterances to them, that
which it only whispered unto others.
Every bird that sung, every scene of Nature seemed to inspire new thoughts and
awaken new aspirations to Se-quo-yah.
Even the wind playing melodies on the
tree leaves seemed to him like words of
the Great Spirit, which his sensitive nature translated into words of wisdom.
Nature was his teacher through which
he lived a life beyond the ken of all other
in the Cherokee tribe. But as the honey
moon wore off, he became more meditative and philosophically inclined, and she
more thoroughly practical. She worked
and he dreamed and thus their lives grew
widely apart. She became a virago and
on many a morning, in later years, the
voice of Se-quo-yah's wife could be heard
giving her lord "Jesse" for the lack of
such industry as she exclusively held in
esteem. "However," says, Boudinot, the

Executive Secretary of the Nation, "he seemed to have taken all his scoldings with great equanimity. No doubt he put himself in her place and made full allowance for the disagreeable prospect from her standpoint." She never was divorced or separated from him. Indeed, except the few years,—those years devoted especially to dreaming—he was her pride. She had considered herself fortunate to secure him in her early days, for he was the general favorite. "The females especially," says one of his biographers, "were attracted by his manners and his skill, and lavished upon him an admiration which distinguished him as the chief favorite of those ever quick-sighted in discovering the excellent qualities of the other sex." Se-quo-yah had a mild, engaging countenance, which naturally would attract. It was destitute of that wild and fierce expression which almost always marks the features, or characterizes the expression, of the American Indian and their descendant. It exhibited

no trace of the ferocity of the savage; it
wanted alike the vigilant eye of the warrior and the stupid apathy of the less intellectual of that race. The contour of
the face and the whole style of expression
were decidedly Asiatic, and might be triumphantly cited in evidenceof the Orien-
tal origin of our tribes, by those who mention that plausible theory. "Indeed", says
one writer," it bore almost a feminine re-
finement and a luxurious softness about it
which might characterize the features of
an Eastern Sage."

CHAPTER VII.

STORY TELLING.

The Pisa Described—Owatoga Dreams—Offers
Himself as a Sacrifice—The Pisa Slain—Cher-
okee and Catawbas wage War—Hiwassee and
Not-ley—Where the Waters Unite—The Fawns—
Success—Hiwassee's Warning—Flight—Reunion
—Marriage—Valley Home—The Story of Okefin-
okee.

> Should you ask me, whence these stories?
> Whence these legends and traditions,
> With the odors of the forest,
> With the dew and damp of meadows,
> With the curling smoke of wigwams,
> With the rushing of great rivers,
> With their frequent repetitions,
> With their wild reverberations,
> As of thunder in the mountains?
>   *   *   *   *   *   *
> I should answer, I should tell you,
> "In the bird's-nests of the forest,
> In the lodges of the beaver,
> In the hoof-prints of the bison,
> In the eyry of the eagle."

> *—Longfellow.*

Se-quo-yah was the famous story teller of his tribe and the legends and traditions recited around the campfires of the Cherokees would in themselves make a volume. Many of them are forgotten, but a few are still preserved, and may be found in early history where mention is made of this people.　Counterparts of many Cherokee traditions are often to be found in the legends of other tribes, especially so in those with which they were allied.

THE PISA.

"Many thousand moons ago, before the arrival of the palefaces, when the great megalonyx and mastodon, whose bones are now thrown up, were still living in the land of green prairies, there existed a bird of such dimensions that he could easily carry off in his talons a full grown deer.　Having obtained a taste of human flesh, from time to time he would prey upon nothing else.　He was as artful as he was powerful; he would dart suddenly and unexpectedly upon some Indian, bear

him off to one of his caves in the bluffs
and devour him. Hundreds of warriors
attempted for years to destroy him, but
without success. Whole villages were
depopulated and consternation spread
throughout all tribes. At length, Owatoga, a chief, whose fame as a warrior extended even beyond the great lakes, sep-
arating himself from the rest of his tribe,
fasted in solitude for the space of a whole
moon, and prayed to the Great Spirit,
the Master of Life, that he would protect
his children from the Pisa. On the last
night of his fast, the Great Spirit appeared to him in a dream and directed him to
select twenty of his warriors, each armed
with a bow with pointed arrows, and to
conceal them in a designated spot. Near
the place of their concealment another
warrior was to stand in open view as a
victim for the Pisa, which they must
shoot the instant he pounced upon his
prey. When the chief awoke in the morning, he thanked the Great Spirit, returned
to his tribe and told them his dream. The

warriors were quickly selected and placed in ambush. Owatoga offered himself as the victim, willing to die for his tribe, and placing his feet firmly to earth began to chant the death song of a warrior; a moment after, the Pisa arose into the air and swift as a thunderbolt, darted down upon the chief. Scarcely had he reached his victim, when every bow was sprung, and every arrow was sped to the feather into his body. The Pisa uttered a wild, fearful scream, that resounded far over the opposite side of the river and expired. Owatoga was safe. Not an arrow, not even the talons of the bird had touched him : for the Master of Life, in admiration of his noble deed, held over him, an invisible shield. In memory of this event, the image of the Pisa was engraved in the face of the bluff."

THE ENCHANTED MOUNTAIN.

A century ago, a bitter war raged between the Catawba and Cherokee tribes of Indians. In one of those frequent and bold excursions common among the wild inhabitants of the forest, the son of the principal Cherokee Chief surprised and captured a large town belonging to the Catawba tribe. Among the captives was the daughter of the first chief of the Catawbas, named Highwassee (or the pretty fawn.) A young Cherokee hero whose name was Not-ley, (or the daring horseman) instantly became captivated with the majestic beauty and graceful manners of his royal captive, and was overwhelmed with delight, upon finding his love reciprocated by the object of his hearts adoration. With two attendants, he presented himself before the Catawba warrior, who happened to be absent when the town was taken by the Cherokees, to whom he gave a brief statement of recent occurrences, and then demanded his daughter in marriage. The proud Catawba, lifting high his war-club, knitting his brow, and curling his lips, with scorn declared, that as the Catawbas drank the waters of the east and the Cherokees the

waters of the west, when this insolent
and daring lad could find where these
waters joined, then, and not till then,
might the hateful Cherokee unite with
the great Catawba. Discouraged but not
despairing, Not-ley turned away from the
presence of the proud and unfeeling father of the beautiful Hiwassee, and resolved to hunt for the union of the eastern
and western waters, which was then considered an impossibility. Ascending a
pinnacle of the great chain of the Alle-
ghanies, more commonly called the Blue
Ridge, which is known to divide the waters of the Atlantic from those of the
great West, and traversing its devious
and winding course, he could frequently
find springs running each way, and having their sources within a few paces of
each other; but this was not what he
desired. Day after day was spent on this
arduous business, and there appeared no
hope that his energy and perseverance
would be rewarded. But on a certain day
when he had well nigh exhausted him-

self with hunger and other privations, he came to a lovely spot on the summit of a ridge affording a delightful plain. Here he resolved to repose and refresh himself during the sultry portion of the day. Seating himself upon the ground and thinking upon Hiwassee, he saw three young fawns moving toward a small lake, the stream of which was rippling at his feet, and whilst they were sipping the pure drops from the transparent pool, our hero found himself unconsciously creeping toward them. Untaught in the rules of danger the little fawns gave no indications of retiring. Not-ley had now approached so near that he expected in a moment by one leap to lay hold and capture one, at least, of the spotted prey; when to his surprise, he saw another stream running out of the beautiful lake down the western side of the mountain. Springing forward with a bound of forest deer, and screaming with frantic joy, he exclaimed, "Hiwassee! O Hiwassee, I have found it." This romantic spot is but

a few miles of Clatonville, Ga. Having
accomplished his object, he at once set
out for the residence of Hiwassee's father,
accompanied only by one warrior, and
fortunately for the success of the enterprise, he met the beautiful maiden with
some confidential attendants half a mile
from her father's house. She informed
him that her father was indignant at his
proposals, that he would not regard his
promises. "I will fly with you to the
mountains," said Hiwassee, "but my father will never consent to my marriage."
Not-ley then pointed her to a mountain in
the distance and said if he found her
there he should drink of the waters that
flowed from the beautiful lake. A few
moments afterward, Not-ley met the Catawba chief near the town and at once
informed him of this wonderful discovery
and offered to conduct him to the place.
The Catawba chief, half choked with
rage, accused Not-ley with the intention
of deceiving him, in order to get him
near the line of the territory, where
the Cherokees were waiting to kill

him. "But", said he, "as you have
spared my daughter so will I spare you,
and permit you at once to depart; but I
have sworn you shall never marry my
daughter, and I can't swear false." "Then
by the Great Spirit, she is mine !" said
Not-ley, and the next moment he disappeared in a thick forest. That night
brought no sleep to the Catawba chief,
for Hiwassee did not return. Pursuit was
made in vain. He saw his daughter no
more. But Not-ley bounding the mountains soon met his beloved Hiwassee, the
marriage was solemnized according to
the custom of their country; they led a
secluded life in those wild regions for
three years, and upon hearing of the
death of his father, Not-ley settled in
the charming valley of the river on the
western side of the mountain and called
it Hiwassee, after his beautiful spouse.
In process of time he was unanimously
chosen first chief of the Cherokees and
was the instrument of making perpetual
peace between his tribe and the Catawbas.

TRADITION OF THE FLOOD.

There is in Union County Georgia, in
the land of the early Cherokee, a beautiful mountain called the "Enchanted."
The country around presents a most charming prospect. The gently undulating
hills are covered by a carpet of richest
verdure—the deep green foliage of the
trees, and the countless varieties of the
most splendid flowers, scattered in gay
profusion over the whole face of the
country, gives it, indeed, the appearance of enchantment. This mountain is
a spur of the Blue Ridge and derived its
name from the great number of tracks or
impressions of the feet and hands of various animals in the rocks, which appear
above its surface. Says a writer in 1834 :
"The number visible or defined is one
hundred and thirty-six, some of them
quite natural and perfect, and others
rather rude imitations, and most of them
from the effects of time have become more

or less obliterated. They comprise human
feet from those four inches in length, to
those of great warriors, which measure
seventeen and a half inches in length and
seven and three quarters in breadth across
the toes. What is a little curious, all the
human feet are natural except this, which
has six toes, proving him to have been a
descendent of Titon. There are twenty-
six of these impressions, all bare save one,
which has the appearance of having worn
moccasins. A fine turned hand, rather
delicate, occupied a place near the great
warrior, and probably the impression of
his wife's hand, who no doubt accompanied her husband in all his excursions,
sharing his toils and soothing his cares
away. Many horse tracks are to be seen.
One seems to have been shod; some are
very small, and one measures twelve
inches and a half by nine and a half.
This the Cherokees say was the footprint
of the great war horse, which their chief-
tain rode. The tracks of a great many
turkeys, turtles, terrapins, a large bear's

paw, a snake's trail, and the foot prints of two deer are to be seen." The tradition respecting these impressions varies. One asserts that the world was once deluged with water, and men with all animated beings were destroyed, except one family, together with various animals necessary to replenish the earth—that the Great Spirit before the floods came commanded them to embark in a big canoe, which after long sailing was drawn to this spot by a bevy of swans and rested there, and here the whole troop of animals was disembarked leaving the impressions as they passed over the rock, which being softened by reason of long submersion, kindly received and preserved them.

OKEFINOKEE.

On one of the many islands of a great swamp lying in the far South, is one of the most beautiful spots in the world. It is inhabited by a peculiar race of Indians, whose women were incomparably beautiful. This place was once seen by hunters when in pursuit of game. They were lost in the inextricable swamps and bogs, and on the point of perishing, when they were unexpectedly relieved by a company of beautiful women, whom they called "Daughters of the Sun," who kindly gave them such provisions as they had, chiefly fruit, such as oranges, dates &c., and some corn cakes. They then enjoined them to fly for safety to their own country as their husbands were fierce men and cruel to strangers. As they left they obtained a view of their settlement situated on the elevated banks of an inland promontory in a beautiful lake; but in all their efforts to approach it they were involved in perpetual labyrinths, and, like enchanted land, when they imagined they had just gained it, it seemed to fly before them, alternately appearing and disappearing. They resolved to leave the delusive pursuit and to return, which, after a number of inexpressible difficulties, they effected. When they reported their adventures to their own countrymen, their young warriors were inflamed with a desire to invade and conquer so charming a country ; but all of their attempts proved abortive, and to this day no warrior has been able to find that enchanted spot, or indeed any road leading to it.

NOTE.—The last two stories in this chapter have been adapted to this work from the Historical Collections of Georgia.

CHAPTER VIII.

AN INSPIRATION OF NATURE.

Se-quo-yah's Native Land—Nature the prime-motor
of genius—The White Prisoner—A Letter—
The Mania to Solve the Mystery of the Talking
Leaf—Se-quo-yah writes on Stone—A Derisive
Laugh—Stung to Action—Dreaming.

Se-quo-yah's young manhood was spent
in a country where Nature was lavish
with her choicest gifts. Across the Cherokee Nation stretched a lofty range of
mountains, even such as Ramond wrote
of whose peaks seemed like beacons
beckoning one from the sins of earth to
the purity of heaven. Of Se-quo-yah's
native land, Ramsey says :—It was the
most beautiful and inviting sectionof the
United States ; a land which those mountaineers of Aboriginal America held onto

and defended with a heroic constancy
and unyielding tenacity which cannot be
too much admired or eulogized." The
Northern part of the Nation was full of
beautiful hills, and there were also exten-
sive and fertile plains. Abundant springs
of pure water were found in every part;
through tall treed forests full of game,
glided most beautiful streams of water,
in which sported abundant fish. In the
Spring the ground was clothed in
Spring's richest dress, and Cherokee
flowers of exquisite beauty met and fas-
cinated the eye in every direction. It is
well to speak thus minutely of the sur-
roundings of Se-quo-yah's early home,
because it appears that in the soughing of
the forest, the singing of birds, the bubb-
ling brooks, the grandeur of scenery and
the influence of nature were the prime
motors to Se-quo-yah's genius.

Says one : "The secret and evidence
of human happiness is written in the
broad book of nature."—

"'Tis to have
Attentive and believing faculties;
To go abroad rejoicing in the joy
Of beautiful and well created things.
To love the voice of waters, and the sheen
Of silver fountains leaping to the sea;
To thrill with the rich melody of birds,
Living their life of music; to be glad
In the gay sunshine, reverent in the storm;
To see a beauty in the stirring leaf,
And find calm thoughts beneath the whisper-
tree;
To see, and hear, and breathe the evidences
Of God's deep wisdom in the natural world."

Nature was always to primeval man the wellspring of his imagination, and imagination, says Stewart, is the great spring of human activity, and the principal source of human improvement. From earliest times, this gift seems to have been bestowed to barbarous man through Nature. Man was first placed in a country, where constantly was going on a seedtime and a harvest. Nature was constantly opening to him new pages in her living book, and it was not, until he had well interpreted the pages of Nature's book, that he was permitted to pass, where the pages were for a moment closed by the frosts of winter. And this faculty of imagination is God-given ; hence, as a writer says :—"we are always yearning after things of beauty and shapes of grace ; always picturing to ourselves things fairer and brighter than those immediately before our vision, always dreaming of the worlds outside or inside of this actual every day world." Indeed, all the grand inspirations of mankind, appear to have been received under the grand and inspiring scenes of Nature. Read the earliest history. It was on Mt. Sinai, while Moses stood surrounded by the grand panorama of Nature, that he received from God the ten commandments, which have since constituted the moral code of the world. It was on the mountains that Jotham received the inspiration of his wonderful parable ; it was on the mountains, that Joshua was inspired to write the law on stone ; it was on the mountains that Jonah received a lesson through a gourd, and it was on the mountain, that beautiful mountain of Olives, that God inspired his son to preach that wonderful sermon on the Mount. It was from the valleys of the Alps, in the cold and darkness of the middle ages, that the first cry of awakening and the first challenge for triumphant liberty went up to Heaven :—

"Here stand we, for our homes, our wives and our children."

Does not history repeat itself?—for not a century ago, amidst the grand mountain scenery .of the old Cherokee country, where Nature wore her wildest and loveliest garb, that to Se-quo-yah, that untutored hero of our sketch, came the inspiration, that led to the civilization of his people.

About the time that Gen. Washington had taken, for the second time, his oath of office as President of the United States and Gen. St. Clair was Governor of the great North West, in one of the skirmishes between the white men and Indians, the Cherokees took a white man prisoner, and in his pocket, they found a crumpled piece of paper, which was a letter from a friend. The shrewdness of the prisoner was such as to lead him to interpret this letter for his own advantage. The story that this talking leaf told filled them with wonder and they accepted it as a message from the Great Spirit. They laid the matter before Se-quo-yah, who was accounted by them as a brave favored by the Great Spirit. He believed it to be simply an invention of the white men.

"Much that red men know, they forget," said Se-quo-yah, "they have no way to preserve it. White men make what they know fast on paper like catching a wild animal and taming it."

But long did Se-quo-yah ponder over the mystery. For weeks and months did he wonder and dream over that "talking leaf." If he engaged in the chase, the longing to solve the problem ever followed him—and in the excitement of war, he never forgot the mystery of that written page. It became the mania of his life, the subject of his thoughts by day, and dreams by night. From this time at every

opportunity, he watched the use of books
and papers in white men's hands. He fre-
quented the Moravian Mission Schools
though he never was a pupil. He simply
observed. The United Brethren by this
time had a prosperous Mission, and Mr.
Blackburn had established his school some
time before this, so that a book was not a
rare thing to obtain. At this time he could
neither read or speak a word of English,
but as luck would have it, Se-quo-yah
came in possession of a whole bundle of
white men's talking leaves, in shape of an
English Spelling Book. Eagerly took he
this to his wigwam, attentively did he listen, and earnestly examine but not one of
the "talking leaves" even whispered to Se-
quo-yah's listening ear of the mystery
they concealed. From a careful reading
of the reported interviews with Se-quo-
yah, it is safe to say, that the germ in his
mind leading to the invention of his alphabet had begun to develop even a decade
of years before the meeting of the young
braves at Sauta,* the story of which can
be found in an early copy of the "Chero-

*In 1820.

kee Phœnix." Some of the young Cherokee braves were one evening reclining
around the campfire, when they began
making remarks about the superior talents
of white people. One said that white men
could put their talk on paper and send it
to any distance, and it would be under-
stood by those who received it. They all
agreed that this was very strange, but they
could not see how it could be done. Se-
quo-yah, whose mind had long since cleared
up from the effect of his life of debauch,
sat there quietly listening. At length he
raised himself and said:—"You are all
fools. I can do it myself. The thing is
very easy," and picking up a flat stone, he
commenced scratching on it with a pin
and after a few moments, he read them a
sentence which he had written, making a
sign for each word. His attempt to write,
produced a laugh from his companions and
the conversation ended. But this laugh
stung Se-quo-yah to action and he put his
inventive powers to work. He was not
content, for nothing short of being able to put the Cherokee language in

writing would now satisfy him; and now comes another link in the long chain of circumstances. How much we are indebted for our fortunes through life's misfortunes. Se–quo–yah met with a misfortune one day, which thereafter deprived him of the glories of war and the excitement of the chase. Then day by day, he sat at his cabin door, listening to the voices of Nature. The "Katydids" scolded at his feet; the "whip-po-wills" called in the forest; the robin would "Cure him, cure him," in the tree top and the "Phœbe" would sing to him, from the dead branch of the maple. And Sequo-yah perceived that feelings and passions were conveyed by different sounds, and often, when he was wearied with his long thinking of that talking leaf taken years before from the captive, he would listen to the song of the birds, the waving grass, the rustle of the oak leaves, and the more measured tones of the needles of sombre pines, and the ripple of the brook until he dozed, and these

songs of Nature often took in his dreams
the form of Cherokee words, and Se-
quo-yah would awake and tell his wife
and children what the leaves of the trees
and Nature had whispered to him in
Cherokee.

CHAPTER IX.

THE GREAT INVENTION.

The Voice of Nature—Picture Writing—Arbitrary Signs—Perfection of the Alphabet—Theoretical—The Scornful Laugh—His Perseverance—"A Prophet not without Honor"—His Final Triumph.

And when he recognized Cherokee sounds in the voice of Nature, there dawned upon his mind a plan by which he could convey this voice to the minds of others, and he sent his sons to the woods for birch bark, and his daughters to the fields for herbs with coloring properties, with which his wife made ink, and with this Se-quo-yah made pictures to represent words. If he found in nature a tone, which he thought represented some word, he drew a picture of that which made the sound. In short, when he thought he had found a sound in nature that represented a tone in Cherokee, he used a picture of this bird or beast, to convey this idea to others, and even his wife and children at first aided him in his work. But this plan, he soon found would be an endless task and instead of these pictures he began to make arbitrary signs. For more than a year, he invented different shaped signs for words until he had several thousand that neither he or any one else could remember. He next hit upon a plan for dividing words into syllables and he found he could apply the same character in different words, and that the number of characters would be comparatively few. He then put down all the words he could think of and then he would listen to the conversation of strangers and for any new syllable, he would make a new character, and here for the first time the talking leaves of the white men first whispered to Se-quo-yah, for several of his characters he took from an English Spelling Book. But these English letters had no relation to their English sound, when used for Cherokee syllables for which they stood. So closely had Se-quo-yah listened for Cherokee sounds, that his first perfected alphabet represented every known syllable of the Cherokee language save three. Who added these to the eighty-two, whether Se-quo-yah or some one else, is not now known; but this remarkable comprehension of a language seems all the more wonderful when we know that before he invented it he could not read. Indeed, it was a wonder to scientific men that a language so copious only embraced eighty-five letters, a single verb often undergoing several hundred inflections. That scornful laugh that stung Se-quo-yah to action, as he scratched his simple sentence on a stone at the evening meeting of the young braves at Sauta, was not confined to the narrow wigwam walls,—for it soon began to echo and re-echo from all parts of

the nation. Se-quo-yah, now a crippled
man, would sit in his native dress at the
door of his hillside cabin, all the time
making strange marks on the birch bark
and paper at his side. The chiefs of the
nation, that once looked up to him, now
passed coldly by, sadly shaking their
heads as they saw the old man's movements. They called him crazy. Friends
and neighbors expostulated with him and
tried to persuade him his acts were fool-
ish, and that none but a delirious person
would do as he did. They called him an
idiot and a fool in Cherokee, but all their
efforts did not discourage him. Slowly
passing his fingers through his now silvered locks, he would listen calmly to
these expostulations of friends, and when
they had wearied he would deliberately
light his pipe, draw several meditative
whiffs, adjust his spectacles and sit down
to his work again, with no attempt at a
vindication of his course. His wife even
began to desert him, being much disgusted at his dreamy ways. His daugh-

ter, however, stood by him, and was always interested in her father's mystic drawings. Still Se-quo-yah persevered. He seemed to have a higher intuition, that the difficulties, hardships and trials of life, the obstacles one encounters on the road to fortune, are positive blessings. He seemed to feel that the Great Spirit never intended that strong and independent beings should be reared by clinging to others like ivy to the oak. He had seen that the toughest plants grew on the peaks of his native hills, and that the weakest grew in sheltered places. For a long time, without a single word of encouragement from any except from his faithful daughter, Se-quo-yah labored until his work was complete. His dreamy meditations on this invention extended from 1809 to 1821, when he completed his work. The last three years of this period he hardly left his cabin, and devoted the whole time to his calculations. That his alphabet was a calculative one is shown by Phillips. He says :—

Se-quo-yah discovered that the language possessed certain musical sounds, such as we call vowels,
and dividing sounds called by us consonants. In
determining his vowels he varied during the progress of discoveries, but finally settled on the six—
a, *e*, *i*, *o*, *u* and a gutteral vowel sounding like *u* in
ung. These had long and short sounds, with the
exception of the gutteral. He next considered his
consonants, or dividing sounds and estimated the
number of combinations of these that would give all
the sounds required to make words in their language. He first adopted fifteen for the dividing
sounds, but settled on twelve primary, the *g* and *k*
being one and sounding more like *k* than *g*, and *d*
like *t*. These may be represented in English as *g*,
h, *l*, *m*, *n*, *qu*, *t*, *dl* or *tl*, *ts*, *w*, *y*, *z*. It will be seen
that if these twelve be multiplied by six vowels,
the number of possible combinations or syllables
would be seventy-two, and by adding the vowel
sounds which may be syllables, the number would
be seventy-eight. However, the gutteral *v*, or sound
of *u* in *ung* does not appear among the combinations, making seventy-seven.

Still his work was not complete. The hiss-
ing sound of *s* entered into the ramification of so
many sounds, as in *sta*, *stu*, *spa*, *spe*. that it would
have required a large addition to his alphabet to
meet this demand. This he simplified by using a
distinct character for the *s*(*oo*), to be used in such
combinations. To provide for the varying sounds
g and *k*. he added a symbol, which has been written in English *ka*. As the syllable *na* is liable to
be aspirated, he added symbols written *nah* and

kna. To have distinct representatives for the combinations rising out of the different sounds of *d* and *t*, he added symbols for *ta, te, ti* and another for *dla*, thus *tla*. These completed the eighty-five characters of his alphabet of syllables and not of letters.∗

Says Gallatin ;—

When the first imperfect copy of that alphabet was received at the War Department, it appeared incredible that a language known to be so copious should have but eighty-five syllables. ∗ ∗ ∗ It would have taken but one step more for Se-quo-yah to have reduced the whole number of consonants to sixteen, and to have had an alphabet similar to ours—by giving to each consonant a distinct character. In practice, however, the superiority of Se-quo-yah's alphabet is manifest, and has been fully proved by experience. You must indeed learn and remember eighty-five letters instead of twenty-five. But this once accomplished the education of the pupil is completed; he can read, he is perfect in his orthography without making it the subject of distinct study. The boy learns in a few weeks, that which occupies two years of the time of our boys. It is that peculiarity in the vocal and nasal terminations of syllables, and that absence of double consonants—more discernible to the ear than to the eye—which we alluded to when speaking of some affinity between the Cherokee and Iroquois languages.

∗Harper's Magazine, Sept. 1870.

"A prophet is not without honor save in his own country." Having invented an alphabet, he found that his people looked suspiciously on his invention; and lame as he was, he went to the Arkansas Territory. where many of the Cherokees had emigrated. While there he taught a few people the way of using his letters, and a man there wrote a letter in the new alphabet to some friend whom he knew in the old Cherokee Country, which Se-quo-yah took back and it was read to his people. They wondered greatly, but were not convinced of the reality of his invention. He showed it to Col. Lowrey,* the Indian Agent, who lived only three miles from his cabin, but he was skeptical and suggested that the symbols bore no relations to the language or its necessities. At last Se-

*This gentleman had learned from the voice of rumor, the manner in which his ingenious neighbor was employed and regretted his supposed misapplication of his time, and participated in the general sentiment of derision with which the whole community regarded the labors of that once popular artisan, but this now despised alphabet maker.

SE-QUO-YAH TEACHING AH-YO-KEH THE ALPHABET.

quo-yah summoned to his lodge the
most distinguished of his tribe. Minutely he explained to them his invention.
His daughter, Ahyokeh, then six years
old, was called in. She was only a pupil
but Se-quo-yah sent her away from the
company, and then he wrote down any
word or sentiment his friends named, and
when they called her in she easily read

"Well," said Col. Lowrey, "I suppose you have
been engaged in making marks?"

"Yes," said Se-quo-yah, "when a talk is made and
put down it is good to look at afterwards."

Col. Lowrey suggested that Se-quo-yah might
have deceived himself, and that, having a good
memory, he might recollect what he had intended
to write, and suppose he was reading it from paper.

"Not so," said Se-quo-yah, "I read it."

The next day Col. Lowrey rode over to Se-quo-
yah's cabin, and the latter requested his daughter
to repeat the alphabet. The child, without hesita-
tion recited the characters giving each the sound
which the inventor had assigned to it, and performed the task with an ease and rapidity that astonished the visitor, and at the conclusion, uttered the
common expression—"Yoh!" with which the Cherokees expressed surprise. He made further inquiry
and began to doubt if Se-quo-yah was the deluded
schemer which others thought him.

them.   The chiefs were astonished, but
they could not believe that this man,
whom they had thought to be crazy for
three years, had really invented anything
that would be of use to the Nation, and
for some time, Se-quo-yah found a coolness among his people, not only for his
invention, but also for himself.   And to
us,   to-day, it seems remarkable, that
even after the value of the alphabet was
known, the missionaries in the Nation,
who were fast translating the New Testament into the Cherokee language, received this invention with coolness, and
even one missionary then put himself on
record by saying, "By the use of this alphabet, so unlike any other, the Cherokees cut themselves from the sympathies
and respect of the intelligent of other Nations." And thus it was, that Se-quo-yah
went sadly, day by day, among his people, knowing that he had at hand the
key to the progress of his people ; how to
induce his people to accept it was now
as great a problem as the invention, but

time always dispels darkness, and so light came at last to the footsteps of Se-quo-yah. The chiefs deliberated. Full well they knew the value of such an invention if it were real, and at last they resolved on a final test. From various parts of the Nation, they selected their brightest young men and sent them to Se-quo-yah that they might be taught. Faithfully Se-quo-yah instructed them and as faithfully did his pupils apply themselves to their task which soon became a most pleasurable pursuit. At the appointed time the chiefs again assembled at the Council Lodge and the Cherokee students were subjected to the most rigid tests, until to the mind of all, no doubt remained concerning the reality and value of his invention.*

*Rev. A. N. Chamberlin, who has always lived among the Cherokees, in a recent letter, gives this account of one of the tests given to Se-quo-yah, as related to him by Wm. Griffin, now deceased.

"The leading men assembling, placed Se-quo-yah and one of his sons at some distance from each other, and had them write sentences as dictated to

Now came the hour of Se-quo-yah's triumph. Even missionaries began, like the poet, to ask—

"How could one treat in such a way a man,
On whom God's hand had plainly been revealed?"

Those, who used to visit Se-quo-yah's cabin to scoff and sneer now came to praise. Young braves flocked around him to receive instruction and the chiefs ordered to be prepared for Se-quo-yah a great feast, at which, in great pomp, they proclaimed Se-quo-yah from the door of the Council Lodge to be Professor, Philosopher, Prophet and Chief and one much favored of the Great Spirit*.

This grand recognition of Se-quo-yah at once made it a popular thing to be able

them and having them carried by trusty messengers, had the writing of each read by the other, and in that manner tested the correctness of his claims. There were many tests imposed, for the people were very skeptical.

*A person observed to Se-quo-yah, "You have been taught by the Great Spirit." He replied :—"I taught myself". He did not arrogate to himself any extraordinary merit in a discovery which he considered as a result of plain principles.

to read and write. Had the Cherokees then naturally indolent, been obliged to have spent long weeks and even years in school, as it would have been necessary to read in English, they would not, as a nation have attempted it; they would doubtless have continued to prefer the chase, rather than to make such an effort, but the alphabet once learned, they could read at once. So simple was this invention and so well adapted was it to the needs of the Cherokee people, that often only three days were required by the bright youth of the race, to learn the whole system, so that they could at once commence letter writing and even teach this system to others. Indeed it is a historical fact, that the enthusiasm of the young men became so great, that they even abandoned in a measure, the practice of archery, hunting and fishing so as to devote more time to letter writing as an amusement, and it is stated by missionaries as a fact, that Indian youth actually went long journeys for the sole pur-

pose of writing and sending back letters
to their friends, and it was not long before a regular correspondence was opened and kept up between the Cherokees
of Will's Valley and their country-men
located five-hundred miles away—and it
must be remembered that this correspondence was carried on by those who a
few months before had no alphabet.

NOTE.— Rev. A. N. Chamberlin in a letter dated Dec. 3d., 1884, says:—"The language has un-
dergone few changes. One character was dropped
out when printing commenced in this alphabet.
There is one now not used. I find in counting
through three chapters, (one in the New and two
in the Old Testament,) where 3,672 letters are used
there are eight that do not occur at all, three only
once, one four times, while there is one used two-
hundred and fifty times, only eleven characters are
used over one hundred times. As to the amount of
good the Alphabet has done our people, it is beyond estimation. At least ten thousand people
read to-day, who could not, were it not for Se-quo-
yah's alphabet. Untold thousands have been led
through it to Jesus."

THE LORD'S PRAYER IN CHEROKEE.

ᎣᎩᏯᏓᎸᏓ ᏣᏓᎳᏗᎡᎯ ᎦᎸᎳᏗ ᎨᏍᏗ. ᎡᏣᏓᏁᏗ ᎨᏒᎢ. ᏗᏣᏁᎸ ᏫᎦᎾᏄᎦᎸ ᎠᏂᎨᎳᎯ. ᏫᏗᏣᎸᏍᏓ ᎭᏓᏅᏕᎬᎢ ᎾᏍᎩᏯ ᎦᎸᎳᏗ. ᏥᏂᎦᎵᏍᏗᎭ ᏂᏓᏓᏆᎵᏒ ᎠᎦᎵᏍᏓᏴᏗ ᏍᎩᏤᎵ ᎪᎯᎦ.

INTERPRETATION, WITH PRONUNCIATION ACCORDING TO THE ALPHABET.

aw gi daw da | ga lv la di ehi | ga lv quo di yu | ge se sdi | de tsa daw v i | dsa gv wi yu hi ge sv | wi ga na nu gaw i | a ni e law hi | wi dsi ga li sda | ha da nv ste gv i | na sgi ya | ga lv la li | tsi ni ga li sdi ha | ni da daw da qui sv | aw ga li sda yv dil sgi v si | gaw hii ga | di ge sgi v si quo naw | de sgi du gv i | na sgi ya | tsi di ga yaw tsi na haw | tsaw tsi du gi | a le tla sdi | oo da gaw le ye di yi ge sv | wi di sgi ya ti nv sta nv gi | sgi yu da ge sge sdi quo sgi ni | oo yaw ge sv i | tsa tse li | ga ye naw | tsa dv wi yu hi | ge sv i | a le | dsa li ni gi di yi | ge sv i | a le | edsa lv quo di yu | ge sv | ni gaw hi lv i | e me n.

TRANSLATION.

Our Father ‖ heaven dweller, ‖ Hallowed ‖ be ‖ thy name. ‖Thy kingdom ‖ let it make its appearance. ‖ Thy will, ‖ the same as ‖ in heaven ‖ [it] is done. ‖ Daily [adj] our food give to us ‖ this day.‖ Forgive us‖ our debts, ‖ the same as ‖ we forgive‖ our debtors. ‖ And do not ‖ temptation being ‖ lead us into [it]. ‖ Deliver us from ‖ evil existing. ‖ For thine ‖ the kingdom‖ is, ‖ and ‖ the power ‖ is, ‖ and ‖ the glory ‖ is, ‖ forever ‖ amen.

1 A, short. 2 A broad. 3 Lah. 4 Tsec. 5 Nah. 6 Weeh. 7 Weh. 8 Leeh. 9 Neh. 10 Mooh. 11 Keeh 12 Yeeh. 13 Seeh. 14 Clanh. 15 Ah. 16 Luh. 17 Leh. 18 Hah. 19 Woh. 20 Cloh. 21 Tah. 22 Yahn. 23 Lahn. 24 Hee. 25 Ss (sibilant.) 26 Yoh. Un (French.) 28 Hoo. 29 Goh. 30 Tsoo. 31 Maugh. 32 Seh. 33 Saugh. 34 Cleegh. 35 Queegh. 36 Queegh. 37 Sah. 38 Quah. 39 Gnaugh (nasal.) 40 Kaah. 41 Tsahn 42 Sahn. 43 Neech. 44 Kah. 45 Taugh. 46 Keh. 47 Taah. 48 Khan. 49 Weeh. 50 Eeh. 51 Ooh. 52 Yeh. 53 Un. 54 Tun. 55 Kooh. 56 Tsoh. 57 Quoh. 58 Noo. 59 Na. 60 Loh. 61 Yu. 62 Tsch. 63 Tce. 64 Wahn. 65 Tooh. 66 Teh. 67 Tsah. 68 Un. 69 Nch. 70 —— 71 Tsooh. 72 Mah. 73 Clooh. 74 Hnah. 75 Hah. 76 Meeh. 77 Clah. 78 Yah. 79 Wah. 80 Teeh. 81 Clegh. 82 Naa. 83 Quh. 84 Clah. 85 Maah. 86 Quhn.

CHAPTER X.

THE MISSION OF JOHN ARCH.*

The Babe of Nun-ti-ya-lee—A Father's Care—Inseparable Companion—Expert with Bow and Gun—A Hero at Home—Ill Luck—Its Results—Life Empty and Void—Joins the Mission School—Career as a Student—Teacher and Preacher—His Journies—Translates Scripture into Se-quo-yah's Alphabet—Death.

In 1797, in that part of the Old Cherokee Nation called Nun-ti-ya-lee, there was born an Indian babe named At-see, that really holds an important place in the story of Cherokee civilization. His mother died when he was yet an infant, and for some reason the father loved the son with an unusual affection, and from the time At-see was deprived of a mother's care, he hardly allowed his offspring to be out of

*The story of John Arch is to be found in the Missionary Herald, also in a Memoir published by the Mass. S. S. Union in 1832.

his sight. The father was one of the
mightiest hunters of his race and, indeed,
the Nimrod of his time. But now when
he hunted his babe was his inseparable
companion. Often was he seen rushing
through the forest in pursuit of wolf or
deer, bearing the boy safely strapped upon
his back, and it was not long before the
son was crazy with delight at the prospect of a chase. Very soon his father
taught him the use of the bow and afterward how to fire a gun, and before he had
fairly reached his teens, he was known as
one of the most expert marksmen and the
"dead shot" of his tribe. He was always
successful in hunting, always killing more
game than his companion.* On his return
home he always received much praise.
How much he took pride in his reputation
will soon be seen. "The last year which
he spent as a hunter," says his biographer,
"he had a poor gun, and then his companion succeeded better than himself, which

---

*It was customary for two to hunt in company,
though each retained without division whatever
game he had himself acquired.

so mortified him that he was ashamed to
return home and so resolved to hunt no
more." In speaking of this period of his
life, five years after, he said, the world
then appeared empty and void; life seemed to him a burden. A deep melancholy
seized upon his spirits and nothing could
afford relief. This was in the year 1818,
just as the Missionaries had opened the
school at Brainerd, which may properly
be called the birthplace of Cherokee civilization. At-see, now called John Arch,
was then twenty-one years of age. We see
again how great a result can hinge on a
simple circumstance. How much are the
Cherokees indebted to that poor gun. He
became so disgusted at the unsuccessful
hunt that he cared not to return to his
home and he joined several of his companions, who were on their way to Knoxville, in East Tennessee. He there met,
incidentally, one of the assistant missionaries among the Cherokees. The missionary soon perceived that John Arch was
desirous of learning to read, and advised
him to apply for admission at the mission

school at Brainerd.   He was so much interested in the prospect thus opened before him, that he traveled through the
woods nearly a hundred miles to find
the missionary school. "His dress and appearance, when he reached B rainerd,
showed at once that he belonged to the
most uncul tivated portion of his tribe; and
he had s pent so many years in savage life
that the missionaries re ceived his applica-
tion with reluctance: but having heard his
story and noticed the marks of intelligence which his countenance exhibited,
they consent ed to take him on trial.

He told them it was the state of de-
spondency into wh ich he had been cast
by his unprosperous pursuit of the chase
during one whole huntin g season, which
was the principal cause of his lookin g
for enjoyment be yond the confines of his
native forests ; and it was his interview
with the missionary at Knoxville, which
had led him to de termine on cultivating
his mind at school.   He said, he had
ne ver been in that part of the nation before, where the school was situated, nor

had he heard of the school, till informed of it in the manner before stated; but he had come with the intention of remaining if possible. He was admitted, and it was not long before he was able to read and write with considerable correctness, and possessing naturally good judgement he was employed with another young Cherokee to assist one of the missionaries in preparing an elementary school book in the Cherokee language, which was afterward printed. He was baptized into full communion with the Church, on the 20th of March, 1820. It was in this year, that a school was opened at Creekpath, and John Arch became an assistant for Mr. Butrick. The school opened with fairest prospects. The people of all ages seemed anxious to learn and a deep religious interest sprung up:—John Arch devoted himself with energy to his work, pursuing it with "judgement, intelligence and delighted animation." He at length returned to Brainerd, where he was engaged as an interpreter. About this

time he took an extended tour among his
people. His fame as a hunter had made
him familiar to many in the nation, and
in this tour, his re-appearance was hailed
with delight, and the Cherokees and even
the chiefs listened to the words he spoke
with more than an ordinary attention.
The Boot and Path-killer insisted on going with him in this tour. At one place
they were invited to the Council House.

Says the Narrative:—"We accompanied Path-killer and the Boot to the
Council-house, about a mile distant.—
This house, if it may be so called, is
simply three roofs, each about thirty feet
long, supported by crotches, and nearly
forming three sides of a square, with a
fire in the middle of the area, and one
nearly under the inner edge of each
roof. Here we found perhaps a hundred
sons and daughters of the forest. Perfect
order and decency were maintained, and
all the visible objects of nature seemed
to unite to render the scene and the season delightful. Above were the sparkling

stars, almost continually stealing my thoughts from these lower scenes to contemplate the amazing grandeur of that Divine Original from whom they borrow all their luster. Around was the dark but pleasant forest, as a strong wall to screen us from the sight of mortals and to shut us out from the noise and tumult of the world. The rustling leaves bade us welcome to their silent retreat. At my right sat John, at my left, the king, and next the Boot, and then, in proper order, all the honorable of the town. At a suitable time the king arose, and addressed the people in a few words. After this John explained the design of the visit, and read our letters from Brainerd and from Chas. Hicks. He afterward spoke on the importance of education, the evil of drinking, &c. After we had finished our discourse, the king desired us, in token of friendship, to shake hands with all the people. They accordingly passed before us, with the Boot at their head. When the ceremony was over, the Boot made a long speech, exhorting all to attend to what they had heard; especially the young men to consider the words their young brother John had spoken, and urged the women who had children to have them educated."

This was a fair sample of the reception of John Arch on his five hundred miles tour. It was after his return, that he spent quite a time near Willstown near the western limits of the State of Georgia. Here he met Se-quo-yah and became interested in his invention. He readily saw its value and determined to put it into practical use. Before this he had assisted one of the missionaries in translating an elementary school book for the Cherokees, which was afterward printed. He continued his good work as preacher teacher and interpreter until late in the season of 1824, when he was taken ill of dropsy. Unable to travel, he at once sat about translating the third chapter of St. John into the Cherokee language. He then wrote it in the syllabic character of

Se-quo-yah. It was received with wonderful avidity, and was copied many
hundred times and read by the multitudes
whom he had visited in his tour, thus
preparing the way for its quick reception
among his people. This was the first
portion of Scripture translated into the alphabet of Se-quo-yah, though it was rapidly followed by other portions. Thus,
as Se-quo-yah had been raised up to
give to his people a written language,
so was John Arch directed by the same
mysterious providence, to accept the alphabet, as a means of at once circulating, while Cherokee curiosity was fully
aroused, those words, which were instru-
mental, as history proves, in numbering
the Cherokee people among the civilized and christianized races of the
world. And this work completed, John
Arch died—died calmly on the 18th of
June 1825. As his friends gathered at
his bedside and told him that in a few
moments, he must pass beyond, a smile
lighted up his countenance, and raising

his hand, pointing upward, he replied,
"Well, it is good," and his spirit passed
beyond.   We believe for such as he—

"Some angel, watchful, kind,
Stoops for the moment from his kindred band,
Reaches through veil of sleep, a pitying hand,
And leads the dreamer forth into a fairer land."

CHAPTER XI.

THE KEY OF PROGRESS.

The Alphabet a National Institution—Suited for
All—The Medal—The "Phœnix"—Its effect on
the Nation—Circulation of Books and Tracts—
The Rapid Growth of Civilized Ways—Laws on
Scandal.

"Oh kindred of the woods
Lift up your heads, for now the sunrise beams
Scatter the mist of darkness and of dreams;
The world is made anew, and it is good."
F. L. Mace.

Having accepted Se-quo-yah's alphabet at the Council, it at once became a
national institution. An early attempt
was made through missionaries to substi-
tute another for it, but the Cherokees
would listen to no such proposal; their belief in its superiority over the whiteman's
could not be eradicated. This the missionaries soon saw, for at that time Mr.

Worcester wrote as follows :—"Speak to them of writing in any other character, and you throw cold water on the fire you are wishing to kindle. To now persuade them to learn another would be in general a hopeless task. Print a book in Se-quo-yah's alphabet and hundred's can read the moment it is given to them*."

While Se-quo-yah sat in his cabin, dreaming out his alphabet, a Mr. Butrick and David Brown had attempted to re-

*The life of Mr. Worcester as identified with the Cherokees has recently been written by a Cherokee girl, Miss Nevada Couch, a member of Worcester Academy, of Vinita. Published for the Institution. He was ordained Missionary in Boston in 1825. He arrived in the old Cherokee Nation on Oct. 21st of that year. He died April 20, 1859. A small, neat shaft of Rutland marble marks the place at Park Hill where the mortal part awaits the last trumpet's call to immortality. On the two sides of the shaft are the names of his two wives. The face bears this inscription: —

"Rev. S. A. WORCESTER, D. D.,

For 34 years a Missionary of the American Board of Commissioners for Foreign Missions among the Cherokees. To his work they owe their Bible and Hymn Book."

duce the language to Roman form and a
spelling book was issued, with which it
was hoped to teach the young Cherokees
to read their language. To teach the
old they supposed would be an impossibility. But a short time after Se-quo-
yah had made known his alphabet, one
of the teachers among the Cherokees
wrote :—"The children of the Cherokees only were thought to be within the
range of our efforts, but as far as the
heavens are above the earth so are God's
thoughts above our thoughts, for we now
see that the objects to which this blessing
is bestowed is not to the children only
but to the fathers and mothers and even
grand-fathers and grand-mothers of the
Cherokee Nation". Thus it was that both
Indians and whitemen paid tardy justice
to Se-quo-yah. In 1824, the Cherokees
in general council voted to Se-quo-yah a

*David Brown was a brother of Catharine, the
first convert under the work of the American Board
in the Cherokee Nation. A memoir of her life and
sketch of the family was published under the aus-
pices of the Board in 1825.

large silver medal as a mark of distinction for his discovery. It was intended that this medal should be formally presented at a council, but two of the chiefs dying and John Ross, who was then their principal chief, being desirous of the honor and gratification of making the presentation, and not knowing when Se-quo-yah would return to the Nation* sent it to him accompanied with an elaborate address, and with due ceremony it was placed around Se-quo-yah's neck and he ever after very proudly wore it.

The medal† had this inscription engraved in English, also in the Se-quo-yan alphabet ;—

"PRESENTED TO SE-QUO-YAH BY THE GENERAL COURT OF THE CHEROKEE NATION, FOR HIS INGENUITY IN THE INVENTION OF THE CHEROKEE ALPHABET."

On one side were two pipes, the ancient symbol of the Indian religion and laws ; on the other was the head of a man.

*He went to the Arkansas Cherokee Nation in Spring of 1823, and never returned again to the old Cherokee Nation.

†This medal was made in Washington.

On February 21st, 1828, not five years
after Se-quo-yah's alphabet had been accepted by his nation, an iron printing
press of improved construction and fonts
of Cherokee and English type, together
with the entire furniture of a printing office was put up at new Echota and the
first copy of the "Cherokee Phœnix" was
given to the world. It was the average
size of the newspapers of that day and
one fourth of it was printed in the Se-
quo-yan alphabet, and all this at the order of the Cherokee Council. This printing press was the first ever owned by any
aborigines of this continent. It was
owned by citizens, who of all the natives
of this continent were the first to invent
and use an alphabet of their own, and,
indeed, it was the first aborigines alphabet, that had been invented for over a
thousand years, and more than this, they
presented to the world the most perfect orthography that this world has ever
seen. The "Phœnix" was the first aboriginal paper on this continent, and Elias

Boudinot, the first aboriginal editor.* In his editorial labors the young Cherokee editor, was assisted often by missionaries. Before the first issue was printed, a prospectus was sent out. "The great object of the "Phœnix" said the prospectus will be to benefit the Cherokees and these subjects will occupy the columns :—1st. the laws and public documents of the Nation ; 2d, Accounts of the manners and customs of the Cherokees and their progress in education, religion and the arts of civilized life, with such notices of other Indians as our limited means will allow ; 3d, The principal interesting events of the day ; 4th, Miscellaneous articles calculated to promote literature, civilization and religion among the Cherokees." Such were the articles that were printed and that Se-quo-yah read in letters of his own invention. Up to about this time it

---

*He was educated at the Mission School at Cornwall, Ct. Married Hattie Gould, a favorite young lady of the village. Was assassinated about 1839. Col. E. C. Boudinot, now so well known at Washington is his son.

had been almost impossible for the Cherokees to be induced to wear a whiteman's dress. Some twenty years before a leading chief was induced to do so, but he was soon laughed to shame and he threw it aside in disgust. About this time, Boudinot the Cherokee editor, who had been induced to wear a civilized dress was often heard to speak of the feeling of shame that wearing this dress gave him, but it was not long before the people became accustomed to and adopted the proper dress of civilization. On the November following the February on which the first copy of the "Phœnix" was published, a missionary wrote, that it was his opinion that at least three fourths of the Cherokee people could both read and write in their new alphabet, and so it was that Se-quo-yah by his alphabet became the great enlightener of the Cherokee people. One year after his death, the Cherokee Nation appropriated $2000 for the establishment of another paper called the "Chorokee Advocate," to be devoted as the prospectus said, "to the moral and intellectual improvement of the Cherokee people." The paper continued until 1854, when it was again suspended. It revived again in 1870, and is now in a prosperous condition, and the official paper of the Nation.*

And the Cherokees were also the first of the Aborigines of this country to present a well organized system for the general diffusion of knowledge. On the introduction of the printing press their craving for knowledge took a rapid stride, and the publications in the Cherokee alphabet were eagerly sought after. "The enthusiasm of the Cherokees is kindled," wrote Mr. Worcester at this time; "great

---

*W. P. Ross was the first editor of the *Advocate*; D. H. Ross was his successor, who was followed by David Carter and James Vann, under whom the paper suspended. After the war W. P. Boudinot took charge. He was followed by Geo. Johnson, and after two years E. C. Boudinot, Jr., was appointed editor. He was succeeded by D. H. Ross, the present editor, who with good editorial ability publishes a paper creditable to the Nation.

D. H. ROSS, EDITOR OF "ADVOCATE."

numbers have learned to read and write. They are circulating hymns and portions of the Scripture; they are eagerly anticipating the time when they can read the white man's Bible in their own alphabet."

Within five years of Se-quo-yah's triumphal recognition, the press at New Echota had turned off 733,800 pages of good reading, which was eagerly read and re-read by Cherokees. Two years after, the number of pages had increased to 1,513,800 and before Se-quo-yah's death about 4,000,000 pages of good reading had been printed in Cherokee, and this not including the circulation of the "Phœnix". Such a general distribution of good literature among a people, where it was so eagerly read could but have a civilizing effect in all ways upon the people. They began to abandon their superstitions; they gradually adopted the whiteman's dress; they put themselves in the way of religious teachings; they began to produce grain for market, instead of raising only for their

own use; they became more frugal; they
favored law, order, morality and temperance. Records show that nowhere in the
Cherokee Nation did the cause of temperance spread so rapidly as in the immedi-
ate vicinity of Se-quo-yah's early home
and it was not long before a missionary
wrote from that vicinity that the traffic in
drink had almost ceased. In an incred-
ibly short time, they doubled the number
of their sheep, horses, cattle and swine;
agricultural implements were in greater
demand; a few sawmills were put up;
public roads established and guide-boards
in Se-quo-yah's alphabet pointed out the
way. Schools were started; Cherokee
women began to weave with looms; the
wigwams gave place to rude huts. When
Se-quo-yah was born, the smoke from
their wigwams ascended through open-
ings at the top, but now, even a few
chimneys were put up with brick. The
Cherokees now tried to imitate the white
men in the management of their affairs;
plows that they had hitherto been unac-

customed to they adopted; instead of appearing nearly, in the clothing that Nature gave them, they appeared in proper dress. The women began to cover their heads, first with handkerchiefs, then with men's hats, and for the first time, on one bright Sunday in 1826, a Cherokee woman put on a new Spring bonnet, and made her first profound sensation. But the funny part of it—which goes to show that history repeats itself—was the fact: during the next month, a male missionary forwarded a report to headquarters in Boston, saying that he "regretted to notice a growing extravagance in dress among the women of the Cherokee Nation." As the great wheel of human progress rolled over the Cherokee Nation, village loafers grew less and less, and the gossiping o'harrigans of the wigwams forgot to lie about their neighbors. God gave to these progressive Cherokees, an intuition that they might be an example of good to the pale-faced gossipers of all

time.   Indeed it now seems, that a man
of ordinary running ability, in front of an
agile Indian, was much safer and more
likely to save his scalp, than he would his
reputation from the wagging tongues of
white gossipers and scandal mongers. Civilized tongue-scalping—it there can be
such a mixture—is infinitely more cruel,
than that done by the Indian scalping
knife.   Many are the reputations blasted
by the wagging tongues of gossipers; the
fair reputation of our daughters, who have
never allowed a blot on their pure page
in God's Record Book, have often been
blackened by the beastly insinuations of
street corner loafers, or from the mouth of
female busybodies, those having a heath-
enish ardor to tell something new and
that something to the disadvantage of
somebody else. All hail the Cherokee law
on slander in force to-day! for the scan-
dal-monger of malicious intent will suffer
punishment by a fine in any sum not exceeding two thousand dollars for the
benefit of the person injured, or by in-

prisonment for a term of not exceeding
two years, or both fine and imprisonment
at the discretion of the Court. Small, pu-
silanimous brats about the villages thought
it not manly to curse and swear. Cherokee youth ceased to irreverently call
their fathers "the old man," even in Cherokee, nor did they disgrace their language
by calling their sainted mothers, "the old
woman". Their thirst for knowledge soon
excelled their love for drink, lewdness
gave way to progress and through the
careful teachings of the missionaries, the
Cherokees learned of a better life.

> "Thine inspiration comes!
> In skill the blessing falls!
> The field around him blooms,
> The temple rears its walls,
> And saints adore,
> And music swells,
> Where savage yells
> Were heard before."

CHAPTER XII.

CHECKS TO PROGRESS.

The Rapacious Whites—Speech of Speckled Snake —Troubles in Georgia—Unjust Laws—Driven out by the Guard—The "Phœnix" Suppressed— Emigration—Trouble and Suffering—Civil War —Their Alphabet now a Key to Progress.

But the impression must not be conveyed, that this Nation became a perfect one. There was, and ever will be much darkness to dispel, much stupidity to be banished, much vice to be restrained. There were many relapses, apostasies, various disappointments for which may God forgive the rapacious white man; when we consider many adverse circumstances, we can only wonder at the result achieved. Just as the Cherokees were beginning to take a prominent stand in civilized ways, the United States was scheming to possess their land and to drive them by fair means or foul from their native soil. No better portrayal of the very shameful condition of affairs, which were agitating the Cherokees at this time, (1830), can be produced than in the reply of Speckled Snake to the speech of President Jackson. It was as follows:—

BROTHERS:—We have heard the talk of our great father; it is very kind. He says he loves his red children. Brothers! When the whiteman first came to these shores, the Muscogees gave him land, and kindled him a fire to make him comfortable; and when the palefaces of the South made war on him, their young men drew the tomahawk, and protected his head from the scalping knife. But when the white man had warmed himself before Indian's fire, and filled himself with Indian's hominy, he became very large; he stopped not for the mountain tops, and his feet covered the plains and the valleys. His hands grasped the eastern and even the western sea. Then he became

our great father. He loved his red children; but said, 'You must move a little
farther lest I should by accident tread
on you.'   With one foot he pushed the
red men over the Oconee, and with the
other he trampled down the graves of his
fathers. But our great father still loved
his red children, and he soon made them
another talk. He said much ; but meant
nothing but move a little farther, you are
too near me.   I have heard a good many
talks from our great father and they all
began and ended the same.   Brothers !
When he made us a talk on a former occasion, he said :—'Get a little farther ;
go beyond the Oconee, and the Ockmul-
gee ; there is a pleasant country.'   He
also said, "It shall be yours forever.'
Now, he says, 'The land you live on is
not yours ; go beyond the Mississippi ;
there is land ; there is game ; there you
may remain while the grass grows or the
water runs'. Brothers ! Will not our father
come there also? He loves his red children and his tongue is not forked."

For some time the state of Georgia
had tried in various ways to drive the
United States Government into her meas-

ures for the forcible possessing of the Cherokee country, and resolved to seize upon the land of the Cherokees under the color of law, but to make those laws so oppressive that the Indians could not live under them. The laws alluded to were passed on the 20th of December, 1829, by the legislature of the State of Georgia. The following is an extract :—

"It is hereby ordained, that all the laws of Georgia are extended over the Cherokee country. That after the first day of June, 1830, all Indians then at that time residing in said territory shall be liable and subject to such laws and regulations as the legislature may hereafter prescribe. That all laws, usages and customs made and established and enforced in said territory, by said Cherokee Indians, be, and the same are hereby, on a nd after the 1st day of June 1830, declared null and void; and no Indian, or descendants of an Indian residing within the Creek or Cherokee nations of Indians, shall be deemed a competent witness or party to any suit in any court, where a whiteman is a defendant."

"Such," says Drake, "is a specimen of the laws framed to throw the Indians into entire confusion, that they might be more easily overcome, destroyed, or forced from the land of their nativity.

That the Cherokees could not live under the laws of Georgia is most manifest, as it is equally manifest that said laws were never made in expectation that they would be submitted to. Thus was the axe not only laid at the root of the tree of Cherokee liberty, but it was also shortly to be wielded by the strong arm of power with deadly effect."

It was not long before the Cherokees were thrown into a state of great confusion, and their thoughts were drawn from advancing in civilization and especially directed toward the preservation of their rights, in the land God Almighty had deeded to them. Only two months after the unholy law just quoted came into effect, the persecutions commenced. Injunctions were decreed by law forbidding the Cherokees to dig for gold on their own land under a penalty of $20,000 ; at the same time white men from all directions were digging unmolested in those very mines.

In 1831, the "Phœnix," the great educator of the Cherokees became the subject of attack. Up to this time it had done its good work as an educator without direct attack, but in its issue of Feb. 19th, 1831, is the following :—

"This week, we present to our readers but half a sheet. The reason is, one of our printers has left us; and we expect another, who is a white man to quit us very soon, either to be dragged to the Georgia Penitentiary for a term of not less than four years, or for his personal safety to leave the Nation, to let us shift for ourselves as well as we can. Thus is the liberty of the press guaranteed by the constitution of Georgia."

At this time there were many noble men engaged in teaching the Cherokees, but even those who were freely giving their lives in this noble work could not be let alone. In March 1831, the "Phœnix" said: —

"The law of Georgia, making it a high misdemeanor for a white man to reside in the Cherokee Nation, without taking the oath of allegiance, and obtaining a permit from the Governor of Georgia, or his agents, is now in course of execution. On last Sabbath, after the usual time of divine service, the Georgia Guard arrived and arrested three of our citizens, viz., Rev. Samuel A. Worcester, Mr. J. F. Wheeler, one of our printers, and Thomas Vann, the last two being citizens, with Cherokee families. Mr. Isaac Proctor, assistant missionary had the evening before been taken, and came with a guard as a prisoner. On Monday they were taken to Etohwah, where were taken the Rev. John Thompson, and Mr. William Thompson."

Such a state of affairs could have no other than a checking influence in their new zeal for civilization, but the desire of many of the Cherokees still was that their children might be educated, and some were already preparing to find a home farther west, to escape the unjust persecutions. In June of the next year, the "Phœnix" said :—

'The gigantic silver pipe which George Washington placed in the hands of the Cherokees, as a memorial of his warm and abiding friendship, has ceased to reciprocate : it lies in the corner of the executive chamber, cold like its author to rise no more.'

In October 1835, Georgia took possession of the "Phœnix ;" further issue was stopped. The same year, a treaty was made by a few not representing the majority of the Cherokee people, whereby their territory was given to the United States in exchange for lands beyond the Mississippi. In 1836, this treaty was ratified at Washington, and orders were given for the Cherokees to leave their country within two years. "At this time," says Bartlett, "there was a singular state of promise all along the line. It seemed as though all things were now ready for one wide ingathering into complete civilization, and into the kingdom of God. Everywhere were centers of light. The traveler would have seen half the Cherokees in Georgia able to read, and leavened with eight churches; while the arts and methods of civilized life were rapidly spreading. There were schools, courts, a legislature, and stringent laws against intemperance and strong drinks."

Such was the condition of affairs when the order to leave the country came.

"The Book of Troubles and Miseries of the Emigrating Indians has not been written," says Drake. "Hundreds have been swept off by sickness on their rugged road ; old and infirm persons fell under the fatigues and hardships of their journey ; hundreds were buried beneath the waves of the Mississippi in one awful catastrophe ; wives left husbands on the way, never more to join them ; mothers were hurried from the graves of their children ; and Mrs. Ross, wife of the great chief of that name, languished and died before reaching the unkown land to which she was bound."

Some of the Indians emigrated early, but the majority clung tenderly to their homes and graves of their fathers. In October 1837, the 31st day, the "Monmouth", a rotten Steamer furnished by the Government to transport some of the Indians up the Mississippi, collided with another and sunk and 311 out of 600 crowded into the old boat were drowned, nor were any requiems chanted, or sorrowing words spoken except by the missionaries, and a few noble men, who recognized in the Indians a god-given soul. On their way across the country

many Cherokees sickened, and from the
result of their removal over 4000 died—
nearly one fourth of the nation. It is
not to be wondered at, under such circumstances, that the attention of the
Cherokees was turned from educational
pursuits. In 1845, the "Advocate" began
its good work and continued until 1854.
About that time new disturbances began to arise and then came the civil
war, the result of which proved to them
a great disaster. About this time, 1861,
the A. B. C. F. M. unfortunately dis-
continued its work among the Cherokees,
and the publication of new religious literature entirely ceased. When the civil
war opened the South demanded the
Cherokees as soldiers and the North demanded them as soldiers. Both North
and South were in honor bound to let
them alone and keep their hands off
their lands and property. Both North
and South joined hands to make of their
houses, ashes ; and their farms grass and
weeds, and again thoughtless minds of

do n't care spirits finished the work left
undone by North and South, so that what
the Cherokees have to day is really the
work of about twenty years.

Many Cherokees were wounded in the
battle of Dec. 1861, and still greater was
the loss in the pursuit. The night after
the battle snow fell to the depth of one
foot or more and the weather became ter-
ribly cold. In the battle and the pursuit
that followed the Cherokees lost most of
their beds, bedding and wearing apparel,
provisions and horses. In such weather
and snow, stripped of almost all they
had, they were forced to find their way
into Kansas ; horses and Indians froze to
death ; hundreds were frozen in their ex-
tremities, of whom some recovered but
many died. During the conflict the Cherokees were robbed by their enemies of
one half of all they had and their reputed
friends did not scruple to take the rest,
and they became literally destitute, so
much so, that in three years after the war
their death rate exceeded their birth rate

by nearly 3,000, and it took nearly a
decade of years for this people to recuperate. The year 1870, will, in the future, prove to have marked another important era in Cherokee progress. The
"Advocate" was re-established and an
effort was once more made to utilize the
Se-quo-yan alphabet. The writers in the
States, on Cherokee matters, have mostly pointed out the mastering of English
as the best way of educating the Cherokee, and in their struggles toward civilization in later years, less attention was
paid to Se-quo-yah's alphabet. On this
point, Wm. P. Boudinot, the Executive
Secretary of the Cherokee Nation, in a
personal letter to the author, writes :—
"In this, I think the Cherokees made a
great mistake. The theory among
certain leading ones was that the less
use made of the alphabet the better, because the English would then super-
cede the Cherokee language more
rapidly—their conclusions being that a
knowledge of English was the first ne-

cessity. So it is, but the theory was wrong, because the cultivation of intelligence in their own language would materially have directed their attention and desire to acquiring English in order to increase their knowledge." In 1869 the National Council so realized the necessity of utilizing still more the Se–quo–yan alphabet, that a committee was appointed to select arithmetics, a geography and history to be translated into the Se-quo-yan alphabet for the use of schools. The importance of such an act can be realized in reading the preface of the Cherokee-English arithmetic prepared in 1870 by the authority of the Cherokee Council. An extract is as follows :—

"It has been deplored that that portion of the children of this Nation who do not speak English have been compelled to lose entirely the benefits of our Public Schools, or else, while attending school to pore, day after day, over lessons of which they could learn only the *sounds*. They have had to endure all the toil and drudgery of study, without that encouragement which comes from the pleasure of acquiring new ideas. Some have attended English schools enough to have acquired a good education, had text books been written and schools taught in their vernacular language. After years spent of most irksome labor, when they had arrived at manhood and womanhood, many of them have found that they had scarcely acquired sufficient knowledge of the English language to begin successfully the study of the elementary branches. It was too late; the responsibilities and cares of life are upon them. Baffled and despairing, they have given over the struggle for an education."

The restoration of the alphabet to popular favor, and printing text books in their own language, has had once more its civilizing effect upon the nation. Still there are no public schools in the nation to-day devoted exclusively to teaching in their alphabet. The simple lessons necessary to enable the full Cherokee to read and write are learned by the fireside and the parents are the teachers. The Nation, since 1880 has furnished the "Advocate" free to all non English speaking members of their race, and in this way they keep well posted on both national and secular affairs.

Se-quo-yah, though born in the darkest period of Cherokee history, lived to see three printing presses running within the nation; he lived until fully 4,000,000 pages of good literature, printed in the alphabet he made, had been circulated among his people; he lived to see school houses and many churches spring up within the nation; he lived to see his people governed by a constitution, which divided the power of government into legislative, executive and judicial departments; a government allowing all free citizens having attained the age of eighteen years to vote at all public elections; a government where the Judges were supported by fixed salaries, and were not allowed to receive fees or perquisites of office, or hold any other office of profit or trust whatever; a government where the right of trial by jury should remain inviolate; where no person, who denies the existence of a God should hold any office in the civil departments of his Nation. Such were some of the laws that Se-quo-yah lived to see adopted by his Nation.

As before intimated, like many of his countrymen, he was early driven an exile from the beautiful land he loved so well, from his field, his workshop and the orchards on that clear stream flowing down from the mountains of Georgia. He joined his countrymen, who had gone West of the Mississippi, and when, in 1828, nine of the principal men of that portion of the Cherokee people proceeded to Washington, D. C., as a delegation from their Nation, principally for the purpose of obtaining a survey of their territory and a deffinite establishment of its limits, Se-quoyah went with them. While there he was the Center of attraction. A "savage," who had developed an alphabet, was to them a wonder. Many were the interviews that politicians, students and learned men had with him through the interpreters Boudinot and Brown. While there his portrait was painted and it still is preserved with portraits of other Indian celebrities of the red race. He then wore his Indian cos-tume and the medal that had been given him by his people. Congress took due recognition then of this now comparatively forgotten genius and as a recognition of his greatness, they declared that the sum of $500 should be given him as a token of appreciation of the benefit he had conferred upon his people in inventing for them an alphabet. So plainly did Congress see the benefits that the Cherokee people were deriving from the alphabet, that they agreed to pay the Cherokees annually for ten years the sum of $2.000 to be expended under the direction of the United States for the education of their children in their own country; also Congress appropriated $1,000 toward the purchase of a printing press and type to aid the Cherokees in their progress in education and to benefit and enlighten them as a people. Such in part was the recognition that the U. S. Congress took of Se-quo-yah and his work in 1828.

CHAPTER XIII.

SE-QUO-YAH, THE MODERN MOSES.

As a Teacher—Again a Dreamer—Would write a
Book—Queer Expedition in Search of Knowledge
Received in Honor—The Last Trip—Sickness—
Death—Vision of the Past and Result of his in-
vention—The Great Conception.

> "'Tis like a dream when one awakes,
>   This vision of the scenes of old;
> 'Tis like the moon when morning breaks;
>   'Tis like a tale round watchfires told."

Se-quo-yah now devoted much of his
time in teaching his invention to his people. He traveled many hundred miles
stopping to teach wherever he could
find a pupil. To impart knowledge and
to spread the fame of his invention now
became his passionate delight. But at the
age of sixty, rheumatism troubled his
wounded knee, and again he sat by his
cabin door and dreamed. It was now

that a grander inspiration seized him.
The voices he now heard in his dreams
were not the songs of Nature. In that
memorable trip to Washington, he had
closely listened to the sounds of the different languages, which he had heard
spoken, and now was dawning on his
mind a theory of a connecting link between them, especially those of Indian
tribes, and strange to say Se-quo-yah
conceived an idea of writing a book. To
him there was no such thing as a studied
Philology. Books to him, with the exception of the "Phœnix," the translated portions of the Bible, the Cherokee Alma-
nacs, songs and hymns were the only
printed leaves that even whispered to Se-
quo-yah. How without the aid of books
and records of the past was Se-quo-yah
to unravel the mysteries of Philology?

Having at last recovered from his attack of rheumatism, he at once put his
plan of collecting materials for his essay
on the "Linguistic Chain"into execution.
There were for him no libraries, with

alcoves of rich lore; there were no musty records or parchments of the past to aid him—the first thing he did toward the accomplishment of his purpose was to construct an ox cart.

One bright morning, in the year 1840, there started out in the Arkansas Cherokee Nation, one of the most peculiar expeditions in search of knowledge that the world has ever known. First and foremost in the company we recognize our friend, Se-quo-yah. He had heard the ancient tradition, that a part of his people were in New Mexico, having been separated from them, some time before the advent of the white race, and somewhere there, he expected to find a missing link in the linguistic chain. And for this purpose, he started westward. With him was a Cherokee boy as a companion, who drove the oxen attached to the rude Indian cart, in which were various articles of use, trade and the tools of his profession—and thus it was that Sequo-yah started in pursuit of knowledge for his book. For two years at least did this queer knowledge crusade travel in the wilds, and though tribes were hostile and at war, Se-quo-yah and his traveling school-house was permitted to pass on in peace. His fame as a philosopher, school master, prophet and chief had gone before him, and as he visited tribe after tribe he was received with honor and they aided him as best they could in his quest for knowledge, and furnished him means also, to prosecute his inquiries in each tribe and clan. Several journies were made, but he wearied not in prosecuting the researches he had commenced. Many were the facts picked up ; many were the proofs collected favorable to his theory. Early in 1842, Se-quo-yah started on his long journey westward and with his traveling school house and College of Mechanic Arts reached a ridge of the Rocky Mountains. He was directed to a pass through which he could drive cart and oxen. He was worn out with his long journies, researches and pro-

SE-QUO-YAH, THE MODERN MOSES.

found meditations on matters for his book.

For a day, Se-quo-yah camped on a spur of the mountains, and before him lay what he supposed to be the promised land where he would find a missing branch of his race. As in early days, the Hebrew, Moses, went from the plains of Moab unto the mountains of Nebo, to the top of Pisgah and was shown the land of Gilead unto Dan, so God permitted the great school master of the Cherokees to leave the plains and to behold the land of his dreams. The Scriptures say, that the Lord buried the Hebrew Moses in the valley, and no one knoweth his sepulchre unto this day, and there arose not another like him—and so it seems to have been God's will in the case of Se-quo-yah. Down the pass, he, the boy, the cart and oxen journied, followed by an admiring retinue. He visited the valleys of New Mexico, looked at the adobe villages of the Pueblos, but found not that for which he sought, and one day, sick of fever, and worn and

weary, near San Bernardino, he halted
his ox cart. Up to this time he had sustained his sufferings with so much fortitude, that his companions realized not
that the end was near, but they gently
bore him to a cave, a fire was built, and
they tried to warm away the chill that
had seized upon his limbs. As the day
drew to a close, it was evident to all that
the last hour had come, and as the sun
passed behind the horizon, leaving its
rich halo behind it, the Cherokee School
Master, Philosopher and Chief quietly
fell asleep.

> "And since the chieftain here has slept,
> Full many a Winter's wind has swept,
> And many an age has softly crept
> Over his humble sepulchre."

Oft they tell us, who are suddenly
borne to the arms of death and are suddenly snatched back to life again, of a
vision of a single moment, containing,
as it were, the whole weal or woe of
life. Thus for a moment, a shade of
sadness darkened the brow of our dying
hero, as there passed before his mental

eye, a vision of the incompleted possi-
bilities of what might have been—a
grand panorama of his great conception and a vision of Cherokee wrongs.

He saw as it were a picture of that
wrong, which was inflicted on his race
by the before mentioned treaty of the
United States, in 1836. He saw then
his nation a happy people, dwelling in a
beautiful land which was to them a home,
the land of their ancestry, the birthplace of their own civilization, and the
burial place of their fathers. Those
little towns on the silvery Chattahooche
and the golden Etowah, were as precious
to them as the villages we love so well;
those wigwams and cabins on the turbid
Ocklacony and the crystal Tugaloo were
as dear to the early Cherokees as are the
homes of any whitemen,—it was the
Cherokees "Sweet, Sweet Home," and
"be it ever so humble, there is no place
like home." And these homes were to be
no more theirs after a few short years,
for it had been so decreed, by the Great

Government of the paleface, that these
homes, and the burial places of their fathers they must leave forever; that the
graves of their wives and little ones could
no longer be their sacred property, but
were hence-forth to be trampled upon and
desecrated by indifferent strangers. One
year passes and still another, but the
Cherokees make no effort for removal;
sadly they see each sun rise and set, and
they know that the hour draws nigh;
they know also that to resist is useless.
Yet they cling to their lands and homes
until the last moment, when on the out-
skirts of the Cherokee Nation on that
beautiful May morning in 1838, there
came on all sides of their Nation, except
the westward the tramp, tramp, tramp
of United States' troops, and the soldiers
began to drive the Cherokees from the
scattered wigwams and cabins on the out-
skirts toward the center of their Nation;
family after family were driven from their
homes before the glistening bayonets of
the white men; for weeks were these Cher-

okees hunted in the woods like wild beasts,
and near the center of the Nation, into
three great herds, like so many cattle,
were 16,000 Cherokee men, women and
children gathered together. What a vision. Three great herds of human beings
called "savages," driven from the land
that God Almighty deeded to them, by
the white barbarians of a so called christian civilization. The heat of the Sum-
mer sun waxed hot; and springs dried up,
so that for some time the march toward
their home in the far west was delayed.
Even before they started many heart-
broken Cherokees fell sick and died and
happily were laid to rest in their native
land. Let, here, the curtain fall. We
cannot depict the sufferings of that long
march across the country; we will not re-
late its horrors; neither will we point out
the path they took—it is marked by 4000
Cherokee graves made new in a short
four months' time, from sickness caused
by hardships and broken hearts. When
did any Indian race massacre in so short
a time so many white men? 16,000 Cher-

okees herded together and driven from
the land God Almighty deeded to them,
and 4000 of these die before they could
reach the far off land deeded to them in
return by the United States.

And still another vision met the eye of
our dying hero, and he saw the grand results of the alphabet he had made. He
saw a race that in a few short years had
made greater progress than any other recorded on History's page,—the result of
his achievment was revealed in a perfect
light—but that which faded from his
view was a completion of his grand conception—a conception so great, that no
human being ever conceived the like
before—that of forming a more wonderful
alphabet, one that would enable all the
Indian tribes of North America to read
and speak a common language, that
would enable them to unite in forming a
grand confederacy, for the purpose of de-
fense ; for their mutual preservation from
the encroachments of the white men, and
their lasting perpetuation in the land
deeded to the Indians by Almighty God.

CHAPTER XIV·

THE ABORIGINES ELYSIUM.

True to the Indian Faith—The Gates Ajar—Beyond
The Gates—The Lost Race at Last—From Dust-
Worn Ruts—Forgotten Benefactors—Among Indian Lore —The Little Book—Its Result—Wonderful Progress.

"Such graves as his are Pilgrims' shrines,
    Shrines to no code or creed confined,—
The Delphian race, the Palistines,
    The Meccas of the mind".

Se-quo-yah died nearly fifty years ago
having attained the age of three score
years and ten, just the alloted age of man.
He died believing fully in that faith his
mother taught him. He died as the good
Indian dies, with all that peace of mind
promised in God's holy word both to
Jew and Gentile. He died happy in the
Indian faith of a glorious hereafter. And
when the last hour came, and his eagle

eye dimmed to the hills, the forest of
strong oak and sombre pines, when
his ear no longer heard the river's mur-
mur and the song of the birds he loved
so well, there came a smile upon his face,
as if there opened to him a door to a sweet
land, even as to our own St. John, the
pearly gates opened to disclose the beauties of a new Jerusalem—as if he beheld
before him the boundaries of an enchanted nation, to which, conscious that he had
lived true to the law that nature taught
him, he approached without fear, look-
ing for no punishment only for reward.
As he crossed the boundaries, another
smile rested on his face, as if grandly
there dawned to him the glories of the
Aborigines Elysium.—A mighty forest
decked with foliage of softest shade, and
carpeted with velvet leaves and silken
needles from majestic pines; verdant
groves wafting sweet perfume on gentle
airs; a shady woods, where warbling
birds in golden plumage carrolled won-
derous melody, where for his silvered

arrow, herds of stately deer and buffalo
idly waited on a thousand ambushed
plains, and where monster fish sported
for him alone in silvery brooks, which
rippled over pebbly beds of gold. And
somewhere, in this happy hunting
ground, he thought to find the wigwams
of those who had gone before, and with
them to live on forever, never growing
old, but in this new world to develope
constantly new capacities. Within the
breast of every lover of justice, let the
fires of indignation burn, for in every
garbled account of Se-quo-yah's life, the
historians have made one point against
him, "induced no doubt," says Phillipps,
"by the narrow minded ecclesiastic, because he would not go through the rou-
tine of a christian profession, after the
fashion they prescribed. Hence they have
scrupled not to say he was a pagan."
Some have affirmed that he died regret-
ting that he had invented an alphabet to
carry the teachings of the white man's
Bible to his people, while one missionary

even that it was only his spirit of rivalry, because he would outstrip the white man, that induced him to invent an alphabet for his people. Be these charges true or not, let their memories be buried with all that is mortal of Se-quo-yah. For what right have we, having found a genius that Providence gave, to raise in his own way a people from their benightedness, to select from the great alphabet of human characteristics a single defect, and brand it as a "Scarlet Letter" against him. Many of these false charges arose without doubt from not comprehending him; for, notwithstanding his genius, the far too conceited whiteman considered him an ignorant savage, while in fact he comprehended himself and measured them. Says Rev. W. A. Duncan, Chairman of the Cherokee Board of Education, in a personal letter to the author :—

"Se-quo-yah, though a "heathen," as Christians would call him, put the key in the missionaries' hands, by which they were enabled to unlock the door

and carry in to the Indian mind the rich
treasures of the gospel. Se-quo-yah gave
them letters, but strange to say, he rejected his religion. He never became a
"convert," but I think God has many
ways of reaching the minds of people
without having to travel along the narrow
path, which our partial knowledge of
the universe is wont to mark out for his
feet. Se-quo-yah sleeps on the banks of
the Colorado, and though the wild flower
has no tongue to tell of the spot doubtless
in the great day, it will be seen that God
found some way to get him to Heaven."

We judge our fellow man too much.
Indeed, what right has one unless a god,
to brand another as among the doomed,
because in his candid, honest search for
knowledge, he may have been haply lifted
from old ruts and had revealed to him
things to him or us unseen before and in
fields and pastures new, boldly starts the
plow of progress, that outside the dust-
worn ruts, in new but god-given fields,
he may reap larger harvests, and cull

new and brighter flowers for God and for
humanity. Should some great record of
man's earthly usefulness be opened to-day
and should we hear proclaimed the result
of his life and ours, who would be able
to stand, even with uncovered head, in
the presence of Se-quo-yah.

"Who loves and lives with Nature tolerates
Baseness in nothing; high and solemn thought
Are his,—clean deeds and honorable life.
If he be poet, as our Master was,
His song will be a mighty argument,
Heroic in its structure to support
The weight of the world forever! All great things
Are native to it, as the Sun to Heaven.
Such was thy song, O Master! and such fame
As only the kings of thought receive, is thine;—
Be happy with it in thy larger life
Where Time is not, and the sad word—Farewell!"

How soon are forgotten the true benefactors of mankind, and how few writers
on American History have thought to pay
even a passing tribute to Se-quo-yah. I
once visited the great bookstores of Boston to consult old books and new, hoping
to find deserved tributes to Se-quo-yah.
In one vast library I found shelves full of

volumes treating of Indian tribes. Eagerly sought I, through the musty pages of each to find some new record of this benefactor of mankind. There were scores of books, with long records of Indians brave in war and distinguished in the chase, but nothing of Se-quo-yah. Four solid hours had I turned the pages of those musty volumes of forgotten lore, and was turning away weary and disappointed, when between two mouldy volumes I spied a little book ; it was new and elegantly bound in gold, the cover folding over and fastened at the side. I was amazed to see such a beautiful little book concealed there among those time-worn volumes, and I pulled it from its hiding place, and behold it was the word of God, the New Testament, printed in the Se-quo-yan Alphabet. Not the rough, unsightly characters,* as were left on the bark or paper, by the stick with which Se-quo-yah wrote, but the same rude letters, never-the-less, smoothed

*See Indian Letter Book.

by contact with the revolving wheel
of time, just as civilization has reduced to
symmetry the coarse hieroglyphics from
which our English letters came. And
this little book had been the means of
carrying to the Cherokee people the di-
rections for a higher life. Do I need
write more, even a single word to con-
vince the reader that God raised up Se-
quo-yah for a purpose, and that through
him, the Cherokees became the most be-
nevolent, moral and intellectual of all Indian tribes ;—and more than this, God
with his wonderful finger of love, touched
the hearts of the whitemen and the members of our Christian churches, and they
borrowed from the Cherokee people the
alphabet that Se-quo-yah made, with
which they formed the "Word of God,"
and they gave it to the Cherokees again
in this new form, and this people, always
in pursuit of knowledge and of light, accepted this new revelation, and thus, the
Cherokee people, in addition to their
morality and intelligence, became the

most christian Indian tribe on the face of
the earth.

"And thou, O Church, betake
Thyself to watching, labor—help these men:
God will thee visit of a surety, when
Thou'rt faithful.

Give—
"Light for the forest child!
An outcast though he be,
From the haunts where the sun of childhood
    smiled,
And the country of the free."

CHAPTER XV.

A GRATEFUL PEOPLE.

Public Services—The Treaty of 1816—Treaty of 1828—The Literary Pension—Still Perpetuating His Name—Literary Societies—District—Bust, —Pictures—Testimonials of his People.

Se-quo-yah was not without recognition by his people in the administration of Cherokee affairs. In 1816, when a treaty was made to perpetuate peace and friendship between the United States and Cherokee tribe, or nation, and to remove all further dissentions which might arise from indefinite territorial boundaries, Se-quo-yah was one of the fifteen delegates sent by the Cherokees. The Commissioners plenipotentiary of the United States uniting in signing this treaty with Se-quo-yah and his companions were Major General Andrew Jackson, General David Meriwether, and Jesse Franklin. This treaty was signed at the Chickasaw Council house on the fourteenth of September, and was ratified at Turkey Town by the whole Cherokee Nation, in council assembled, on the fourth day of October. The chiefs and warriors, who signed the ratification were Path Killer, The Glass, Sour Mush, Chulioa, Dick Justice, Richard Brown, The Boot, Chickasawlua. As has been mentioned in a previous chapter, Se-quo-yah was one of the delegates to the City of Washington, in 1828, and was then a signer, as a Chief of the Western Cherokees, to the articles of Convention concluded on the 6th of May. Four of this delegation, Se-quo-yah, Thomas Maw, George Marvis, and John Looney signed these articles in the Se-quo-yan alphabet. On May 31st, at the Council Room, Williamson's Hotel, in Washington, Thomas Graves, George Marvis, Se-quo-yah, Thomas

Maw and John Byers ratified the articles
of Convention. We find no other of-
ficial acts of Se-quo-yah recorded up to
the year 1838. Then the two branches
of the ancient Cherokee family had by
force of circumstances been brought together again; it seemed necessary for
the general welfare that a Union should
be formed and a system of government matured, adapted to their new condition, Se-quo-yah, as President of the
Eastern Cherokees, was a signer of the
act of Union. At this time he made his
"mark," why he did not write his name
in his own alphabet is now a question.
Among the signers of this act of Union
was Jesse Bushyhead, father of the present Chief, and John Benge, whom A. N.
Chamberlin says, became so much interested in Se-quo-yah, while he was making
his alphabetical calculations, that for
some time, he furnished him with writing material to record his meditations.

In 1841, as Se-quo-yah was traveling
in the West, hunting for the lost branch

of his race, an act was passed at the Council giving him a literary pension equal to the salary of a Chief. It was subsequently changed to read as follows:—

AN ACT

FOR THE BENEFIT OF GEORGE GUESS.

Be it enacted by the National Council, That in lieu of the sum allowed to George Guess, in consideration of his invention of the Cherokee alphabet, passed December 10th, 1841, and which is hereby repealed, the sum of three hundred dollars be paid to said George Guess out of the National treasury, annually, during his natural life.

Be it further enacted, That in case of the death of George Guess, that the same be paid to his wife, Mrs. Guess, annually, during her natural life.

TAHLEQUAH, December, 29, 1843.

Approved.   JOHN ROSS.

Though Se–quo–yah never realized any actual benefit himself from this pension, it was paid to his wife and children for many years. And when it was learned that he was really dead, Congress as well as the Cherokee Council thought to bring back his remains and erect over them a suitable monument; but the matter was too long delayed, and when the messengers were

sent out from his Nation to hunt for his
grave, they failed to discover his resting
place. It is not impossible, that in some
future day, some traveler, student or ex-
plorer, in searching in some of the rocky
caverns along the Colorado, for traces of
silver or gold, shall find there a heap of
human bones, the skull of which will indi-
cate, that he who died there, was a man
of more than common intellect. Should
the finder be a phrenologist, he might
stoop to study the skull and to wonder at
the revealed capacities, and then, perhaps,
as he holds his lamp nearer to this funeral
pile, he may see something like a silver
coin just where there was once a human
heart—and it may prove to be the silver
medal given to Se-quo-yah by his race—
unless this happen, the last resting place
of Se-quo-yah will never be known.

Literary Societies, for such gatherings
are not now unusual in the Nation, still
take the name of their benefactor, and
parents still perpetuate his name by be-
stowing it upon their children. One of
the nine districts into which the Nation is

CHEROKEE COUNCIL HOUSE.

divided for government is called after him.

A traveller in the Cherokee Nation to-day, stopping at Tahlequah, their National Capital, would see a large brick structure of excellent architecture and finish. Less than a century ago, this people held their National deliberations in the woods with the tree-branches for shelter, but now they point with a just pride to this imposing structure and say, "This is our Nation's Council House!" And in this Council House is a room set apart for the deliberations of the Board of Education, and in this apartment, the visitor, unacquainted with Cherokee history, points to a marble bust, and asks "What white man is this that the Cherokees thus honor in marble?" And then some Cherokee, with face glowing with enthusiasm and National pride will say, "This is no white man; this is Se-quo-yah, the Cherokee; the pale face can preserve in marble, the memory of the 'Father of his Country'; a Cherokee in the same way honors the

'Father of Learning,' to his people, and this bust, a token of gratitude, was carved at the order of the Cherokee Council.'

From all parts of the Nation to-day there rises up a voice of gratitude and praise. Many Nations have warriors, but Cadmuses are few. "Fathers of a Country" are usually made through war, blood and conquest, but the "Fathers of Learning," receive their inspiration from God; and such seems to have been the case with the great School Master of the Cherokees,

> "Long live the good School! giving out
>   year by year
>   Recruits to true manhood and woman-
>   hood dear:
>   Brave boys, modest maidens, in beauty
>   sent forth,
>   The living epistles and proof of its worth."

CHIEF BUSHYHEAD.

CHAPTER XVI.

A LAW ABIDING PEOPLE.

The Cherokee Constitution and Government—Chief—Judiciary System—Courts—Jurors and Jury Trials—Laws on Treason and Conspiracy—Murder—Immorality—Intemperance—Recognition of the Sabbath, etc.

By the Cherokee Constitution, the supreme executive power of this Nation is vested in the Principal Chief, who holds his office for four years. The present Chief, D. W. Bushyhead, is a son of Jesse Bushyhead, who was one of the first native Baptist Cherokee preachers in the old Cherokee country. Of the father of the Chief, the History of Baptist Missions says:—"He was a convert of superior intelligence and worth. He had learned christianity from the teachings of the Bible alone, and apart from all other instructors had embraced the salvation which it offers with an intelligent conviction and earnest faith, which combined with his own superior understanding rendered him a christian of no ordinary stamp. He was baptized by a minister from Tennessee in 1830, and three years after was ordained to the ministry."

From the time of his conversion up to the time of his death in 1845, he devoted himself to the welfare of his people.. He translated the Genesis, and it was printed in the alphabet of Se-quo-yah. He was accounted one of the most energetic men of the Nation to which he belonged "He was one of the early pioneers of civilization and one of the noblest exemplifications of christian character ever produced."

He was appointed Chief Justice of the Cherokees after their arrival in their new territory, and in this station, which he still held at the time of his death, through many trying periods of National affairs, he was always distinguished for his wise administration of even-handed justice.

It is not the purpose of this work to

discuss in detail, the acts of the present
Principal Chief, that belonging properly to another volume.*   Suffice it to say
that, as his father lived, in a measure,
ahead of his race, so to the eye of a historian, Chief Bushyhead has not confined
his administration solely to present needs.
His administration in coming years will
be seen to have held an important bearing on the future of the Cherokee race.
There may be those in the Nation, who,
taking a narrow and contracted view of
the present, and with no discerning eye
for the future, may fail to catch the bearing of some of the Chief's most important acts.   What better school system can
be shown than that organized under his
administration?—a system equal to that
in vogue in the States, and one that well
followed will command for the Cherokees
both the attention and respect of the
most cultured white man.   What might
have been the future of the Cherokee
race, had not the present Chief caused to
be filed an authentic register of all Cher-
*"A Nation Within a Nation."

okee citizens, thus striking as it were a
death blow to the hope of any who would
by cunning art and sly device blot out
this "Nation within a Nation." Chief
Bushyhead, would long ere this have
collected the scattered historical records
of the past, and had them put in proper
shape for preservation, had not unwonted
obstacles been thrown in the way, by
those who should have sustained him in
his laudable endeavors for the welfare of
his people. Every true hearted Cherokee, should demand that the history
of their race should be fully written.
There is nothing in it of which to be
ashamed. What matters it if early customs were crude, uncouth, and to us to-
day unseemly? It is the story of these
rude customs of old contrasted with the
attainments of the present, that makes
their history grand, inspiring almost un-
precedented. Were we a Cherokee,
we would insist that some loving heart
should search the musty records of the
past, and then, with artist pen, trace the

picture of the race as it was in the days of primitive simplicity. Then would we bid that same artist depict on another canvas, at its side, a picture of the attainments of their race to-day. We would then command him to paint still another picture—the picture of wrongs inflicted on the Cherokees by the white man, and all the checking influence. Then would we command him to trace a historical painting of the progress in the States. First there must be a picture of rude log huts supplanting Indian wigwams; then a view of early and crude life of the early whites in the forest. Then were it possible, we would have him paint the good fortune that has fallen to the white race, that has given to him the blessings and the comforts of civilization and then, beside all, would we bid him trace on the canvas, the result of the whiteman's "Century of Dishonor". toward the red race;—and then we would ask: "Why, O Cherokee, do you hesitate to have your history written, and your annals preserved?"

The Principal Chief is to the Cherokees what the President is to the United States. By their Constitution, no man is eligible to the office of Principal Chief unless he is a native born citizen and he must be at least thirty-five years of age. He visits each district twice each year to acquaint himself with the needs of the people which was a commendatory demand of the Constitution. The acquaintance thus made with the necessities of the Nation aids him in governing wisely and well. He signs and vetoes bills, and sees to it that the laws are faithfully executed. He has around him a Cabinet or council composed of five persons, which he has power to assemble at his discretion and with the Assistant Principal Chief, and councillors, may from time to time hold and keep a Council for ordering and directing the affairs of the Nation, according to law.

On September, the 6th day, 1839, the

Constitution of the Cherokee Nation, with exception of a few amendments, was adopted, as it now stands. To this George Guess, or Se-quo-yah, was a signer. His signature upon that document refutes the only serious charge ever brought against that wonderful man—that he was a pagan. Every recorded act of Se-quo-yah proves that he was not a searcher for fame or glory for himself. It would have been inconsistent with his whole career to have affixed his name to a document that he did not fully understand and in which he did not fully believe. He may have rejected some dogmas of the whiteman, but there is no proof but what he was true to the laws of right that the god of Nature taught him. By thus affixing his name to this document, the Cherokee Constitution is a living refutation of the charges made against him. 'Tis true that he signed no church creed. Yet the Constitution he signed understandingly and in good faith was a creed broad enough to refute the stigmas the narrow minded would bring against him. By signing the Cherokee

Constitution he professed a belief in God and a future state of reward and punishment; for, says their Constitution—

SEC. 1. No person who denies the being of a God, or future state of reward and punishment, shall hold any office in the civil departments in this Nation.

By signing the Constitut ion, he placed himself before the world as an endorser of religious worship ; for, says—

SEC. 2. The free exercise of religious worship, and serving God without distinction, shall forever be enjoyed within the limits of this Nation : *provided*, that this liberty of conscience shall not be construed as to excuse a cts of licentiousness, or justify practices inconsistent with the peace and safety of this Nation.

By signing the Constitution, he proclaimed himself a lover of Justice:—

SEC. 7. The right of trial by jury shall remain inviolate, and every person, for injury sustained in person, property or reputation, shall have remedy by due course of law.

And by his signature to Section 9, Article VI, he stands on record as a champion for the three great factors of Civilization—Religion, Morality and Knowledge.

SEC. 9. Religion, morality and knowledge, being necessary to good government, the preservation of liberty, and the happiness of mankind, schools and the means of education shall forever be encouraged in this Nation.

Section 7 was a clause in the red man's National Constitution adopted in 1839. In 1830, nine years before, the whitemen of Georgia passed a law that "no Indian or descendant of an Indian, residing in the Creek or Cherokee Nations of Indians, shall be deemed a competent witness where a white man is a defendant".

Again, we ask, "Why, O Cherokee, do you not demand that your history be written?" And what think you, O white man? Were not the words of the Immortal Wirt prophetic? when he said over a half century ago:—

"The faith of our nation is fatally linked with the existence of the Cherokees, and the blow which destroys them quenches forever our glory: for what glory can there be of which a patriot can be proud, after the good name of his country shall have departed? We may gather laurels on the field of battle, and trophies on the ocean, but they will never hide this foul blot on our escutcheon. 'Remember the Cherokee Nation,' will be answer enough for the proudest boasts that we can ever make. I cannot believe that this honorable court, possessing the power of preservation, will stand by and see these people stripped of their property and extirpated from the earth while they are holding up to us their treaties and claiming fulfillment of our engagements. If truth and faith and honor and justice have fled from every part of the country, we shall find them here. If not, our sun has gone down in treachery, blood and crime in the face of the world; and instead of being proud of our country, we may well call upon the rocks and mountains to hide our shame from earth and heaven."

When we mention that Wirt lived long enough to see that deep stain fall upon the escutcheon of his country's honor, which he so much feared, we see why all American History is so silent concerning the Cherokees.

Their elections are conducted in as decorous manner as in the States, actually putting to shame some gatherings for a similar nature in the States. For the purpose of government the Cherokee Nation is divided into nine districts called Se-quo-yah, Illinois, Canadian, Flint, Saline, Going-snake, Tahlequah, Coo-wee-scoo-wee and Delaware, and in these districts there are forty-seven voting places authorized by law and these districts are allowed to elect in all forty men as Representatives to the Council, who are entitled to $3,00 per day for their services. Eighteen Representatives to the General Council of the Indian Territory, by the people, and one other is elected by joint vote of the National Council, and commissioned by the Principal Chief. The term of membership of the General Council is two years. The Upper House of the National Council is styled the Senate of the Cherokee Nation. The election of Principal Chief, Assistant Principal Chief, members of the National Council and minor officers takes place on the first Monday in Aug. The Council convenes on the first Monday in November. Before election, the clerk of each district has already promulgated a writ or proclamation of the Principal Chief for the information of the qualified electors of his district. At least ten days before election he has caused to be published by pasting up in some conspicuous place at each and every precinct in his district the names of all persons put in nomination for office, and candidates frequently mention their candidacy in the "Advocate," their National paper. If a male has reached the age of eighteen years, and has been a resident of the Nation for six months immediately preceding the election, if he has not been convicted of felony, if he is not insane, or "non compos mentis" he is considered qualified as a voter. On election morning there is a general assembling at the various voting places. The polls are open before eight o'clock in the forenoon and are kept open until sunset of the same day, an intermission of an hour being taken at noon. Before the opening of the polls a space of fifty feet is marked off encircling the polls, within which no person except the officers of election are allowed to come, except for the purpose of voting, and then but one voter is allowed to enter at a time and he must promptly retire beyond the prescribed limit.

Before the day of election two clerks and two superintendents of election for each precinct are appointed, one of whom must be able to speak both Cherokee and English, and they are selected equally as may be from the opposing candidates. When the superintendents are qualified, with as much fairness as possible to the opposing candidates, they choose three suitable persons to act as supervisors. The polls being open, one of the superintendents proclaims the fact in a loud voice to the voters present, and states what offices are to be filled. He then exposes for inspection of the legal

voters who are present, the rolls then
to be used to show that no names of the
voters are recorded thereon. The rolls
are headed "Returns of election held on
the——day of——at——precinct, in——
district in the Cherokee Nation." These
rolls are ruled with the necessary space
to record the names of the voters and the
names of the candidates, and the votes
each candidate may receive. The voter
then enters the enclosure, and states in
audible voice, the name of the candidate
for whom he desires to vote. The clerk
then records the name of the voter and
places his name to the candidate designated by him, while the second clerk
watches carefully to see that no mistakes
are made. No superintendent, supervisor
or clerk of election are allowed to influence or bias the voting of any voter by
word, deed or other manner, except by
challenge of the legality of a vote. If
there is evidence of a person being an unqualified voter, the clerk or superintendent at once swears the suspected voter,

and a rigid examination of his eligibility is made. The election is carried on with the greatest decorum. To the supervisors are given full authority to preserve the peace during the election, and attend to counting of the votes, and making up the returns. They suppress the sale or indulgence in intoxicating drinks by destroying such liquors, and cause arrest and removal from the precinct, of any drunken or disorderly persons. They make the greatest effort to preserve the purity of the ballot. Should one unqualified cast a vote, or should one vote more than once for the same candidate, not only would he be subject to a fine of not less than $100, and at least a six months' imprisonment, but would be forever disqualified from voting. Bribery is subject to a fine of not less than $100 or over $500, or the offender can be both fined and imprisoned; and if a person by violence, threats or riotous conduct attempts to disturb or break up any election, or unlawfuly prevent the free use of the

elective franchise, or attempt to intimi-
date any candidate for office, he is liable
to a fine of $100 and an imprisonment
of twelve months, and if the offense is
committed by three or more persons
armed with any deadly or dangerous
weapons they are deemed guilty of treason, and upon conviction are made to
suffer death by hanging. The utmost
care is taken of the rolls; at the noon re-
cess, the superintendents and clerks remain in company and in possession of the
rolls. At sunset as the polls are finally
closed, and before leaving the room in
which the election has been held, the superintendents and clerks sum up the
votes cast at the precinct, and the number for each candidate, and continue
without adjournment until the work is
complete. After the result is obtained
the rolls are signed, sealed and properly
marked as election returns from——precinct. On the following day, the superintendents of election of the several pre-
cincts assemble at the regular place of

holding court in each district and deliver
the returns to the clerk of the district,
who in the presence of superintendents,
opens and counts the vote and issues a
written certificate of election to the fortunate candidate. The returns are then
carefully sealed and re-marked election
returns from——district. They are then
placed in the hands of a sheriff or his
deputy, who delivers them in person to
the Principal Chief at the seat of Government. We have been thus minute in regard to the management of their elect-
tions for in no better way can we show
how just is their claim of being a law-
abiding people.

The Judiciary system is divided into
supreme, circuit and district courts. The
supreme court consists of three Judges,
one of whom is selected by a joint vote of
the National Council as Chief Justice.
The power of the supreme court is about
the same as the power of a similar body
in the States ; the decision made has the
force of law. The Judges have and ex-

ercise exclusive criminal jurisdiction of all cases of manslaughter, and in all cases involving punishment of death ; this court has exclusive jurisdiction of all cases instituted to contest an election held by the people, and brought before the court as provided by law : they also have power to award judgements, order decrees, and to issue such writs and processes as they may find necessary to carry into full effect the powers vested in them by law. There are three judicial circuits known as the Northern, Middle and Southern, and one Judge is elected for each circuit. The circuit courts have jurisdiction of all criminal cases, except those of manslaughter, involving directly or indirectly a sum exceeding one hundred dollars, and all civil suits, in which the title to real estate or the right to the occupancy of any portion of the common domain shall be in issue, exceeding one hundred dollars. There is also a district court for each district, for the trying of all criminal cases, whether felonies or misdemeanors, involving the sum of one hundred dollars or less.

No man is allowed as juror, who is under 21 years of age, nor any person, who may be under punishment for misdemeanor, and no member of the legislative or executive departments, or any commissioned officer of the Nation, officiating minister of the gospel, physician, lawyer, public ferryman, school teacher or one older than 65 years is compelled to serve on jury or as guard. Five persons constitute a jury in the trial of all civil suits, any three of whom may render a verdict. In case of manslaughter, twelve jurymen are required, but in all other cases the jury consists of nine persons, and no verdict is rendered in any criminal case without consent of the whole jury. The grand jurors are selected with especial care from the best and most intellectual men of the nation. Their term of service is for one year unless discharged. Five men are summoned from each district for this purpose.

Having thus briefly referred to their excellent Judiciary system, for the benefit of those, who insist on calling all Indians "lawless," it seems best to call attention to a few Cherokee laws which are continually enforced in their nation. It is a lamentable fact, that so large a proportion of the people, in the New England States at least, are so ignorant of the state of civilization this people have reached. Students in our Universities have expressed surprise to know that there are such institutions as Cherokee Seminaries of Learning, and the writer has been warned more than once, to never visit this people, as the scalping knife might do its deadly work. Yet, how can we blame these students and these men so intelligent in other things, when we call to mind the fact that no author has taken pains to write the progress of this people. Indeed, how can we expect honest, fair or intelligent legislation concerning Indians, when all the literature we receive, except that provided by Indian Associations, goes to prejudice the people. As an unprejudiced historian

beholds the Cherokee people to-day, he
sees no longer the tomahawk or the scalping knife; that they were used is only revealed in archives and fading memories of
the past. On the other hand, he reads the
Cherokee law, that every killing of a human being, without authority of law, by
stabbing, shooting, poisoning, or other
means, or in any other manner, is either
murder, or man slaughter in the first second, or third degree, according to the intention of the person perpetrating the act,
and the facts and circumstances connected
with each case. If such killing is done in-
tentionally or by premeditated design, the
person convicted of doing the same suffers
death by hanging; if done without design
to effect death, procurement or culpable
negligence of a person the imprisonment
is not less than two years. Abortionists
are imprisoned for not less than two or
more than ten years; seconds and medical
advisors, in prize fights, where death oc-
curs are deemed guilty of manslaughter.
The careless or avaricious ferryman, who
overloads his boat so that it sinks or en-

dangers the lives of passengers, and every
captain, engineer or other person, in charge
of any steamboat, or other steam power,
where neglect or carelessness results in the
explosion of a boiler and death results,
is deemed guilty of manslaughter. These
laws are rigidly enforced, and there are not
so many cases of assault, murder or manslaughter by the Cherokee people to-day
according to population as in many of the
States. Rape is punished by imprisonment from ten to twenty-five years, and
the ravishment of female children is punished by hanging, a law that might well be
on the statute book of, and enforced in,
every state in the Union. From five to
fifteen years' imprisonment is the punishment for arson, and if death results from
the fire, death is the prospective punishment. Executions take place within the
enclosure of the National prison at Tahlequah, by the high sheriff or some one appointed by him for the purpose.

The first Cherokee Execution by hanging was
in the old Cherokee country in 1828. The unfortu-
nate was a Creek residing in that nation He was

tried for murder one Friday, condemned about
noon and executed on Saturday between the hours
of 12 M. and 1 P. M.   The story goes that "the Jury
were all in tears when they brought in their verdict
and the Judge was very much affected when he pro-
nounced the sentence. All men, women and children fasted from the time he was condemned till after the execution, and most of them were engaged
in praying, singing and exhortation.   The prisoner
took an active part in the devotional exercises. He
stood in the cart under the gallows and delivered
an affecting address, after which he joined with
the people in singing a hymn, which they sung at
his request; he then kneeled down over his coffin
and prayed. He died like a warrior. 'My friends,'
he said, 'I want you to look at me and take warning. My bad conduct and wickedness have brought
me to this afflictive situation. * * Now I leave you
and die. Our Saviour died for poor sinners. I am
not afraid to die.'"

Marriage and divorce are now subject
to law with as much strictness as in the
States. It was in 1826, that the first marriage took place according to christian
usage, in the old Cherokee nation, and
the ceremony was performed by a missionary of the American Board and hundreds of Indians flocked together to see
what was to them a wonderful ceremony.

While Indian Agents, in their reports have sought to make prominent the customs of some in lower grades of Cherokees,—for there are all grades of Cherokees just as there are all grades of white men—we find but little said in regard to the better condition of affairs. If a Cherokee youth has reached the age of eighteen years, and the maiden of his choice has passed sixteen Summers, they are deemed capable of contracting marriage, for now, instead of marriage being a matter of trade or barter, on the part of the parent, as in the days of Se-quo-yah's parents ; or being a matter of gift-bestowing, as when Se-quo-yah took his first wife, marriage is now considered as a civil contract, in which the consent of parties is essential. These marriages are solemnized by any of the Judges of the Courts of the Nation, by the clerks of the several districts, by the ordained ministers of the Gospel in regular communion with any religious society, or, any marriage contracted in writing in the presence of two witnesses, who shall sign the marriage contract, is considered lawful. Reports of all marriages must be filed with the clerk of the district. No marriage can be contracted while either of the parties has a husband or wife living, nor between persons of kin nearer than first cousins, and a heavy penalty is inflicted on any who join minors in marriage, without the consent of parents. Divorces are regulated by law and are adjudged for adultery, imprisonment for three years, for wilful desertion or neglect for a term of one year, for extreme cruelty, or habitual drunkenness for one year. The Cherokee people have always as a nation favored temperance, and have an effective prohibitory law upon the statutes. There is also an act of Congress forbidding the introduction of liquor into the Indian Territory. The United States law, lays a penalty against any white-man or Indian who brings the liquor across the line into the Territory, for any purpose whatever. The Cherokee laws lay a penalty upon the sale of any liquor after it is brought into the Nation. A person may be guilty of one of these offences without being guilty of the other. There is a live organization of the Woman's Christian Temperance Union, which is not backward in reform work. A copy of the compiled laws of 1883 before the writer has the following :

"Be it enacted by the National Council, That lot No. 4 in block 20, in the Town of Tahlequah, be and the same is hereby granted to W. A Duncan, John W. Stapler, John Ross Jr., and William Johnston, they constituting the business committee of 'Tahlequah Christian Temperance Union,' and to their successors in office, for the purpose of building theron a public reading room and library."

Well might some of the States follow the example of the Cherokees in aiding the Temperance Unions in erecting these shrines of virtue.

The violation of the Sunday law, which declares Sunday shall be a day of rest within the limits of the Cherokee Nation, is punished by a fine in any sum not exceeding $50., for each offense, and no merchant, mechanic, artist or other person shall open his store, warehouse or other place of business, or shall engage in any manner of work except by necessity or for charity, without being deemed guilty of misdemeanor. To the reader, it must now be evident, that the Cherokees are indeed a law-abiding people, and these laws must certainly be looked upon with interest and respect by all civilized nations of the world.

CHAPTER XVII.

PUBLIC INSTITUTIONS.

Schoo ls—Seminaries—Revenues—Asylums—Prison—Churches, etc.

> "I said to cold Neglect and Scorn,
>   Pass on—I heed you not;
> Ye may pursue me till my form
>   And being are forgot;
> Yet still the spirit which, you see
>   Undaunted by your wiles,
> Draws from its own nobility
>   Its high-born smiles."

The Cherokees being the first of the
Aborigines tribes on this continent to es-
tablish a free system of schools, it is well
for a moment to examine into their school
system, and note the wonderful progress
this people have made. At present they
have one hundred public schools and two
higher seminaries of learning, and this
not including mission schools of which

there are several. The management of
their public schools is vested in a Board
of Education, consisting of three persons
of liberal literary attainments, who
are free from immoral habits, who are
nominated by the Principal Chief and
confirmed by the Senate. The appoint-
ment covers three years of service, one
dropping out and one being appointed
each year. The Nation is divided into
three school districts, and a member of
the Board is appointed for each. The
Board have complete supervision and
control of the orphan asylum, seminaries
and primary schools, examine teachers,
prescribe courses of study, and to visit
the schools. The full term of study in
the primary department covers three
years, and that in the seminaries four
years. The Board of Education furnish
tuition, clothing, board and lodging to
the children of the primary department
gratuitously, and have full control of
the children while attending school
and until they have completed their term

of study.   They furnish gratuitously, tuition only, to other persons attending the
seminaries, but provide board   at actual cost, the pupils being required to furnish their own bedding and clothing.   A
Board of Directors are appointed for the
primary schools, who control the school
property, take care of school books, libraries, look after erection of buildings, re-
pairs, etc., suspend or expel pupils, and
also visit the schools twice each term
and make necessary reports. The school
year consists of two terms, one of twenty
and one of sixteen weeks.   Preference
is given always, qualifications being
equal, to teachers who are citizens of the
Nation ; hence nearly all of the teachers
are Cherokees.   The pay of teachers in
the primary schools is $35 per month.
The pay of teachers in the Male and Female Seminaries is as follows :—

Principal teacher,	$800
Assistant teachers each,	500
Primary teachers,	300

All schools in the Nation are supported

by money invested in United States reg-
istered stock from the sale of lands to
the United States Government. The interest alone of this investment is drawn
and used for educational purposes. The
United State Government renders no assistance to the Seminaries, Asylum and
common schools of the Nation, outside of
paying interest on money borrowed from
the Nation. The Cherokee National
Male and Female Seminaries were both
founded by act of the Cherokee National
Council, Nov. 26, 1846, which reads as
follows :—

"*Be it enacted by the National Council*, That two
Seminaries or High Schools be established, one for
males and the other for females, in which all those
branches of learning shall be taught, which may be
required to carry the culture of the youth of our
country to its highest practical point."

The buildings were erected and the
Seminaries opened the 7th of May, 1850.
Were we writing of the white race, it
would not seem necessary to publish any
part of their school course, but as it is,
as a kind of an astonisher to those who

persist that the civilization of an Indian
tribe is an impossibility, we give below
a partial li st of studies in the upper classes
in the Female Seminary.

SENIOR CLASS.

First Term.	Second Term.
Virgil.	Evidences of Christianity.
Mental Philosophy.	Mental Philosophy.
Geometry.	Geometry.
Gen. History and Reading.	{ Geology. Astronomy.
Composition.	Composition.

JUNIOR CLASS.

Nat. Philosophy.	Moral Philosophy.
Literature.	{ Botany. Chemistry.
Cæsar.	Virgil.
Algebra.	Algebra.
Composition.	Composition.

SOPHOMORE CLASS.

Rhetoric.	Rhetoric.
Latin Grammar, etc.	Latin Reader.
Arith. Problems.	Algebra.
Ancient History.	Physical Geography.
Composition.	Composition.

FRESHMAN CLASS.

Pract. Arithmetic	Pract. Arithmetic.
Mental Arithmetic.	Zoology.
Grammar.	Analysis.
U. S. History.	Physiology.
Composition.	Composition.

In the last report of their efficient Board
of Education we read:—"It will re-
quire time—may be years, to perfect the
school system so as to accomplish the
highest results, nor is the Cherokee Nation singular in this respect. In the most
favored States, the question as to the best
methods of school work is still an open
one. It is receiving the attention, not only of the educator, but also the philosopher and statesman. * * There are
many obstructions in the way of the
schools of the Nation. The public institutions of a country are but the outgrowth
or product of the sentiments of the people. Even the pyramids are to be taken
as an index to the spirit and purposes of
the Egyptians, and as the sentiment of
the Cherokee people is the soil out of
which the school must grow, it is impossible for them to accomplish the highest
good, until that soil has been so cultivated
as to transmit to them the elements essential to their growth and prosperity. Not
that our people do not appreciate educa-

tion ; they do appreciate education. The only fault is such as is common to mankind. They do not bestow upon education the attention which its real merit demands. When we reflect that the age in which we live is a time when Nations shall rise against Nation for the mightiest achievements the world ever saw and that such achievements are to be won not by the sword, but by the agencies of untrained intellect, we could most sincerely wish that the whole Cherokee people be inspired with a love for education that would at once remove all obstructions, and fill the school houses all over the land with the young people of the country. To say that "the pen is mightier than the sword," is simply saying that reason triumphs when physical force is wanting. Why then should the schools of the country not be considered too sacred to be touched by any deleterious influence? Why not bring to their aid every facility which money can buy? Why not employ for them every device which genius can invent? All depends on them, as far as the future is concerned."

Says W. T. Adair, M. D., the National Medical Superintendent :—"Our institutions of learning are destined to represent a most potent factor in the struggle for future recognition 'among the powers that be.' In a word they are the "safety-valves of our National existence ; for it is here that we must raise up, and train our future patriots and statesmen. It is here the hands must be strengthened, and the intellects stored with the knowledge necessary, at no distant day, to take hold of and conduct the affairs of state—as said before, the question of our dissolution or onward course must rest for settlement with the coming men and women of our race, and if matters so pregnant must be determined by our children, how important it at once becomes, and how solemn the duty devolving on the present generation, to properly educate and train them."

The foregoing extracts go to show

something of the spirit with which the educational matters are carried on and discussed in the Nation to-day, and nearly one fifth of the whole population are enrolled in the public schools.

As before intimated, the "Advocate" is a national institution ; one fourth of the paper is printed in Se-quo-yah's alphabet as required by law. It is furnished free to all non-English speaking Cherokees. As it prints the laws in both English and Cherokee the whole Nation is well informed in respect to law. Rev. A. N. Chamberlin, the interpreter writes : "I presume there is no people anywhere better informed than the non-English speaking Cherokee in regard to their laws and their treaties with the United States." About $4000 is appropriated by the Council annually for the "Advocate" and national printing. The matrix for the Se-quo-yan type is kept in custody of the Nation, and the full Cherokee is in no danger of being corrupted by vicious literature.

The Cherokee National Prison at Tahlequah is under the Superintendence of the "High Sheriff of the Cherokee Nation." Here prisoners are confined, employed or kept in solitary confinement. The prisoners are given wholesome diet but no luxuries, not even sugar or tea. Religious service is frequently held in the prison, and all due means taken to fully reform the prisoner. The Nation have an Asylum for the insane and indigent, blind, deaf, dumb and decrepit, which is under direct control of their government. It is a handsome building and admirably superintended. A well organized Orphan Asylum, for many years, has been an important humane institution. Its object is to constitute a home for the Nation's homeless, where they may receive parental care and affection, and at the same time be placed within the facilities necessary for an academic education.

The funds for carrying on these works are derived from the interest on the resources of their Nation, which in 1884 was reported by the Chief as follows:—

Total National Fund		$1,822,935.55
"	School Fund	1,402,584.57
"	Orphan Fund	994,855.65
. "	Asylum Fund	196,969.61

In 1877 the figures were given as:—

Total National Fund		1,008,285.07
"	School Fund	532,407.01
"	Orphan Fund	175,935.31

Among the more recent institutions for Cherokee civilization is the Teachers' Institute, that meets annually at Tahlequah. This is doing a good work for the higher culture of the Nation. It is under the supervision of the Board of Education, and all the teachers in the Nation are not only obliged to be present, but are expected to take some part in the proceedings. The Superintendent, Rev. W. A. Duncan, is the prime mover in all these gatherings, and a most valuable program of subjects to be discussed is prepared. In the call for the Institute of 1885, Mr. Duncan says:—There is an august future awaiting our country, and to act with wisdom we should prepare ourselves for its largest enjoyment."

CHAPTER XVIII.

THE FAIR LAND.

Location—The Surface—Productions—Statistics—Recuperative Powers—Missionaries—Never-the-less a Cherokee Civilization—Oconnostota's Prophesy.

The Nation of which we have written is located in the North Eastern part of the Indian Territory, the area covered being 7861 square miles or 5,031,351 square acres. The surface of the country north of Tahlequah, the capital, is mostly a rolling, grassy prairie, with a light sandy soil and timbered only along the streams, and devoted mostly to stock raising. On the east of Tahlequah, along the Arkansas line, the country becomes

hilly, broken and rocky. Southeast of
the Illinois is the highest and most mountainous parts, well timbered, the surface
growing less mountainous toward the
Arkansas line, and there are large areas
of good and tillable lands. Westward of
the Illinois the country is hilly and broken. Southward of the Arkansas, in
the angle formed by it and the Canadian,
the country is mostly open and hilly.
The Cherokees occupy and own perhaps
the best reservation among the five civilized tribes. The lower lands, or those
adjacent to the water courses, being susceptible of raising all kinds of grain,
while on most of the prairie land small
grains can be raised with profit. The
grounds surrounding the hewed log cabins, frame or birch or stone houses, are
many of them adorned by ornamental
trees, shrubbery and flowers. There are
many orchards of choice fruit, some of
which have existed for twenty years and
are today in fruitful condition. As we
have before mentioned the Cherokees

came out of the civil war with absolutely nothing. At that time less than two hundred cattle could be found within the nation. "When the war closed," says Ross, "there was not a hog or a foot-print of one to be found in the country." But the recuperative powers of the Cherokees have always been wonderful indeed. More than 14,000 horses, 1,300 mules, 750,000 cattle, 160,000 swine and 15,000 sheep are owned by the Cherokees to-day. Of the 2,500,000 acres of tillable land, 90,000 is cultivated by Cherokees, whose yearly productions approximate to 65,000 bushels of wheat, 750,000 bushels of corn, 55,000 bushels of barley, 44,500 bushels of vegetables and 750,000 pounds of cotton. Examining the Statistical Reports for 1882, the enumeration of the people is given at 20,336, of which over 19,000 adopt citizen's dress, 16,000 speak English, 3,800 Cherokees are engaged in Agriculture and 400 in other civilized pursuits, and none engage in hunting for a livelihood ; 4,500 Cherokee

houses dot the beautiful and fertile lands;
62 churches are lending their ameliora-
ting influence, Baptist, Methodist and
Presbyterian leading the way; 33 missionaries are devoting their time to doing
good among the people. Some of these
missionaries have been there for many
years, and their influence for good is
great. Their means of support are small,
they work hard, and only those remain
in the field who possess the true missionary spirit. The Cherokees contribute
about $2,000 annually for benevolence.
In 1878 the Nation had 60 schools; today
these important factors of civilization
number 100. Says Armstrong: "The
Five Nations, as a whole, are an illustra-
tion of missionary work, which commenc-
ing seventy years ago, with savages,
has in two generations produced as high
a stage of Christian civilization as could
be expected. It is far weaker than that of
the Anglo Saxon, which had its growth
of a thousand years. There is not a
blanket or a wild Indian among them;

they have been humanized; they are
clothed, right minded, intelligent, live in
good, decently furnished houses, and
are self supporting." Says Walker:—
"The Cherokees are of all Indian tribes,
great and small, first in general intelligence, in acquisition of wealth, in the
knowledge of useful arts, and in social
and moral progress. The evidence of a
real and substancial advancement in
these things are too clear to be ques-
tioned." It is no argument against the
Cherokee Nation that the white men
there may be the greatest crop produc-
ers, and that some white men there engage in mechanical pursuits; or · that a
Cherokee can engage a white man to
till the soil, and himself live on the rent-
al; if it is, then the Southerner, who
himself doing nothing, and renting his
lands to, or hiring the negro, must be
looked upon in the same light; the Cali-
fornian must even be accused of barbarous tendencies when he hires the China-
men to do the labor that he might do

himself, or the New Englander, who
hires the honest Irishman, or rents his
lands to him, could with equal propriety
be accused of becoming barbaric. Indeed
it is not to the discredit of the Cherokee
that circumstances have made him, thus
in a measure, an aristocrat, though that
these things are so may be a cause of
jealousy to the avaricious white man. If
things were otherwise it is true that the
people would be more industrious;—and
it is indeed true that lasting greatness is
the outgrowth of constant industry. But
like most any white man the Indian loves
such ease in life as circumstances will
allow. The state of affairs in the Cherokee Nation so severely handled in 1878
by Otis should be looked at not with the
eye of prejudice, but by the light of reason. The Cherokees, naturally indolent,
have become in point of fact, an industrious people, while the descendents of the
old stock white race in the States, naturally industrious, seem to be growing
more indolent. It has taken thousands

of years for the whites to attain their present state of civilization, while the first germs of Cherokee civilization reach back hardly a century. It is no discredit to the Greeks that they owe their letters to Cadmus, a Phœnician. By accepting and making good use of them, the Greek civilization was no less Grecian. It is no discredit to America, that she accepted the services of a Frenchman, Lafayette to help fight the battles of the Revolution. By it America's victory was no less American. English, Scotch, German and Irish intermarry in the States, and their offspring go to make up the American people, who compose our civilization, yet we do not hear it cited that our civilization is any less American that it is so ; neither should the prejudiced or jealous say that the Cherokee Nation is less a Cherokee civilization because whitemen and white women have intermarried with the race.

In closing the first volume of "Cherokee History Series," the eye of the Author rests on a letter written him by a well educated Cherokee lady within the Nation, who traces a clear line of descent from Oconnostota, a celebrated Chief of early days. She says:—"This fair land of ours is a beautiful and fertile flower garden, fresh from God's hand attractive beyond description. Its beauty brings us innumerable dangers." And this remark is true; for the whiteman has always looked with avaricious eye on the "fair land" of the Cherokees, and intruders are always creeping in to possess the land. Methinks, O Cherokee, that thy Ancient Chief, Oconnostota was, indeed, inspired by the Great Spirit, when in 1775, he made that famous talk before thy people; when with earnest words and strong appeal, he spoke those words of warning. Of the insatiable desire of the paleface for more land he said:—

"Whole nations have melted away in the presence of the paleface, like balls of snow before the sun, and have scarcely left their names behind, except as imper-
fectly recorded by their enemies and de-

stroyers. It was once thought, that they would not be willing to travel beyond the mountains, so far from the ocean on which their commerce was carried on. But now that hope has vanished; they have passed the mountains and settled on the Cherokee lands, and wish to have it sanctioned by a treaty. When that is obtained, the same encroaching spirit will lead them upon other lands of the Cherokees; new cessions will be applied for, and, finally, the country which the Cherokees and their forefathers have so long occupied will be called for, and the small remnant, which may then exist of this nation once so great and formidable, will be compelled to seek a retreat in some far distant wilderness, there to dwell but a short space of time, before they will again behold the advancing banners of the same greedy host, who, not being able to point out any further retreat for the then miserable Cherokees, would then proclaim the extinction of the whole race."

The first part of the warning prophesy was long since fulfilled; the latter comes not yet to pass.

Guard well, O Cherokee, thy lands. Let not that worse fate befall thy people—the extinction of thy race.

Remember the warning of Oconnostota in 1775!

Remember the words of thine other countryman, Capt. John Benge, who some thirty years ago said in his broken English, alluding to the sale of "neutral land," —"Yes, sell this piece's of a tract's of a land's and away by'm by sell another piece's of a tract's of a land's and after a while have no lands."

Remember the words of Duncan, thy educator of to-day, who says: "Selling of land in any way, and to any extent is absolutely incompatible with the continuance of Cherokee existence as a people. To sell land is to destroy our nationality."

Let every whiteman remember the admonition of the gifted Frelinghuysen, who said:—"Let us beware how by oppressive encroachments upon the sacred priviliges of our Indian neighbors, we minister to the agonies of future remorse."

Kind reader speak more kindly of our Indian Brothers now that you know them better.

ADDENDA.

[Page 34.]

The custom of the Eastern Cherokees
of burying their dead and heaping upon
them piles of stones and other articles,
and the fact that the early Cherokee woman used to hang fresh food above the
totem of her husband's grave-post is
beautifully expressed by Longfellow,
where the Ghosts come back from Pone-
mah, the Land of the Hereafter, and
sing this song to the miraculous Hiewa-
tha :—

"Do not lay such heavy burdens
On the graves you come to bury,
Not such weight of furs and wampum,
Not such weight of pots and kettles;
For the Spirits faint beneath them.
Only give them food to carry,
Only give them fire to light them.

Four days is the Spirit's journey,
To the land of ghosts and shadows;
Four its lonely night encampments.
Therefore, when the dead are buried,
Let a fire at night be kindled,
That the soul upon its journey
May not grope about in darkness."

[Page 35.]

The early Cherokees ascribed to the Great Spirit the intention of making men immortal on earth; but, they said, the sun, when he passed over, told them there was not room enough, and that people had better die! They also said that the Creator attempted to make the first man and woman out of two stones, but failed, and afterwards fashioned them of clay; and therefore it is that they are perishable.—SQUIER, Serpent-Symbol, p. 67, note c.

[Page 50.]

The popularity of the game of ball was very great. The numbers attending them were very large. Intoxicating liquor became so frequently vended at them, that in 1825 the Cherokee Council, assembled at New Town, passed a law prohibiting the sale of liquors at all ball plays, and night dances.

[Page 53.]

Cherokee conjurers still exist in the Eastern Cherokee Nation. Mrs. Davis in Harper's Magazine says :—

"Crossing one of the heights the Doctor's party came upon old Osoweh, the conjurer, lying flat upon his stomach. He had marked out lines on the muddy ground, and was driving in bits of ash roots here and there. He did not look up as they halted.

'There he has all the countries of the world,' said the interpreter, a nimble young man. 'Where he drives in a peg it rains: where he takes it out the sun shines.'

Mr. Morley laughed. 'Who would expect to find humbuggery on the top of these mountains?' he said throwing a quarter to the wizard. The old man with reddish eye glared vindictively at him a moment, then he turned back to his pegs, but he did not look at the money.

' Now he will send you a storm,' said the interpreter.

'Nonsense, this drouth is going to last for a week.'

The writer humorously adds :—

"But before they had reached the bottom of the next chasm the clouds did actually gather, and a heavy rain began to fall. The shadows of the mountains lay like night over the valley, and the steep, clayey trail became so slippery that even the sure footed mules slid and staggered on the edge of the precipice."

Superstition still exists in the Western Cherokee Nation, though perhaps to not much greater extent than among some classes in the States. An instance is recorded in their national paper in 1885, of a woman who insisted that the ceiling of the house would turn black directly after her decease. This was fully believed by some, and reported to be the fact directly after her death. The National paper mentioning the rumors, facetiously promised to give full particulars in the next issue if the matter did not prove a canard. As no further mention was made of the fact it is to be concluded that this woman was not as successful in her witchery as the Eastern Cherokee conjurer was in the narrative before mentioned.

[Page 68.]

The buffalo hide was a symbol of protection to the early Cherokee. Hence it was often given as a pledge. Worn by the ardent lover of the tribe, it was the mute offer of protection to the maid, whom he would invite to preside over his wigwam, in the same way that the eagle feather was symbolical of his love.

[Page 96.]

"The names of animals given by the early Cherokees, were imitations of the sounds they produced; the names of the trees signified the sound they appeared to make, thus making the name a description of the thing,—according to what is believed to be the primitive origin of names. Thus "see" indicates the sound of waters upon the rocks, and "sahse," the combination of waters. It was found on making up the alphabet for the Cherokee dialect that f, l, r, v and x were excluded. These gentle savages at the end of a word made a liquid note resembling our vowel a ; this produced a flowing sound compared best perhaps to the flow of water. Many Cherokee names of rivers are very beautiful."

———

"Ye say that all have passed away,
    The Noble race and brave—
That their light canoes have vanished
    From off the crested wave ;
That 'mid the forests where they roamed,
    There rings no hunter's shout ;
But their name is on your waters,
    Ye may not wash it out."

Ye say their cane-like cabins
    That clustered o'er the vale,
Have disappeared as withered leaves,
    Before the autumnal gale :
But their memory liveth on your hills,
    Their baptism on your shore ;
Your ever rolling rivers speak,
    Their dialect of yore."

———

"The Names of these rivers" says a a well known writer, "stands the land-marks of our broken vows and unattoned oppression ; they not only stare us in the face from every hill and every stream that bear those expressive names, but they hold up before all nations and before God, the memories of our injustice."

GEORGIA'S RIVERS.

From her mountains on the Northward,
  How do Georgia's Rivers go?
How to Southern Gulf and ocean,
  By her islands do they flow?
From the silvery Chat-ta-hoo-chee,
  And the golden Et-o-wah;
To majestic, broad Sa-van-nah;
  By the grim Al-la-pa-ha;
From the turbid Oc-lo-co-na;
  To the crystal Tu-ga-loo;
From Ches-ta-tee to Cha-too-ga—
Georgia's rivers come and go.

Northward, Tennesse, Hia-was-see,
  Not-ley and Tuc-co-a pour;
Here's U-laf-fie's liquid laughter;
  Here's Tu-ro-ree's toss and roar:
Here's Tu-lu-lah's leaping terror;
  So-que, and the Ap-pa-lach-ie;
Little, Broad, Al-co-fau-hatch-ee:
  San-te, and the Au-chee-hatch-ee;
Coo-sa-wat-tee with its clatter,
  Sal-la-coa and El-li-jay;
Oos-ta-nau-ia, Can-na-san-ga,
  Five in Coo-sa roll away—
Here O-gee-chee and the Med-way,
  And the dark San-til-los creep
Through the barren and the cypress
  And morasses wide and deep,
Thro-na-dee-sca scampers Southward,
  And Can-nou-che's murky tide;

Here's Oc-mul-gee, Tal-la-poo-sa,
  And Al-tam-a-ha the wide—
Oc-o-pil-co and O-co-nee
  And O-co-ee, bright and small ;
With-la-coo-chee and We-law-nee
  Chick-a-saw, and all—
From the Chattering Chat-ta-hoo-chee,
  To Sav-an-nah's splendid flow—
Where is heard the Oo-hoop-ee—
  Georgia's Rivers come and go."

R. V. Moore in Harper's Magazine (Rearranged).

[Page 110.]

It is somewhat remarkable that in all
the alphabets of the world, there is
no authentic information concerning the
inventor of any alphabet except that of
Se-quo-yah. In this volume, he has been
called the American Cadmus, but he was
greater than Cadmus. The Greeks ascribed the invention of their alphabet to
Cadmus, the Phœnician, who planted a
colony at Thebes. By this, however, we
are only to understand, that Cadmus was
the first who made alphabetic characters
known in Greece. That in early days
he was not regarded as the actual inventor is clear ; for Plato, the most learned
of the Greeks expressly said that Thaut,
the Egyptian, was the first that divided
letters into consonants, mutes and liquids

and the Phœnician historian, Sanchoni-
anth further says that Thaut was the inventor of letters.

[Page 145.]

In 1861, the A. B. C. F.M. discontin-
ued its work among the Cherokees, for
reasons stated by the Prudential Committee as follows :—"The Committee regard
the appropriate work of the Board among
that people as having been so far accomplished, and the future prosecution of its
labors as at the same time so far impeded
by the intervention of other denomina-
tions better suited for operating there than
ourselves, as to render it expedient for
the Board to withdraw and to expend the
funds hitherto devoted to this field in
other more needy portions of the unevan-
gelized world." At the close of their labors they still had stations at Dwight,
Lee's Creek, Fairfield and Park Hill.

[Page 161.]

Even the traveller from foreign lands
while enthusiastic regarding the beauties
of that home of the Cherokees becomes
haunted there by the ghost of former
wrongs there inflicted. Robert Somers,
the English traveller and author says:—
"The country presents all phases, from

Nature in her sternest and proudest to Nature in her softest and mildest moods. It seems philosophically to have only two draw-backs, inasmuch as it was founded by the dispossesion of one race, and the subjugation of another." And he might have added,—it was the men of the South that drove the Cherokees from their moun-tain homes, by force of arms in 1838, and by a retributive justice, the men of Southern Blood were themselves driven before the bayonet of Northern troops in 1863.

———

[Page 164.]

It was the general belief among the In-dian tribes, and among the early Chero-kees, that the future life and its avoca-tions are similar to those of the earthly life. In the "Legends of the Dead," we find this attributed to the Cherokees. It was the "Lover's Vision of the Happy Island." The lover had reached the cab-in on the shore of the unknown lake, and freed of his body by the gate keeper, "He bounded forward as if his feet were winged. He found, as he thus sped forward, that all things retained their natural colors and shapes, except that they appeared more beautiful; the colors being richer and shapes more comely; and he would have thought that everything was the same as heretofore, had he not seen that the animals bounded across his path with utmost freedom and confidence and birds of beautiful plumage inhabited the groves and sported in the waters in fearless and undisturbed enjoyment. As he passed on however, he noticed that his passage was not impeded by trees and other objects; he appeared to walk directly through them. They were in fact the souls of trees. He then became sensible that he was in the 'Land of Shadows."

[Page 210.]

Among the very earliest records concerning the Cherokees is to be found a formal expression of a desire to become educated. Dodsley's Annual Register, published in London, England in 1765, had the following under date of Feb. 17. —"The Right Honourable, the Earl of Hillsborough, touched by the very mean and deplorable condition in which he found three Cherokee Indians, lately arrived in London, immediately took them from the hands of a tavern-keeper and a Jew, who had advertised them to be seen for money at the tavern-keeper's house, sent his trade's-men and there equipped them genteelly in the English fashion at his own expense. And this day they were introduced, by Mr. Montague, the agent for Virginia, to the lords of trades and plantations; and with their usual solemnity had four talks with their lordships; the first complimentary; the second to tender obedience to the great king their father, and to produce samples of gold, silver and iron ore, found in their country; the third to complain of the encroachments of some of his majesty's subjects on the hunting grounds reserved by treaty for the sole use of the native Indians; and the fourth to express their surprise that having often heard of learned persons being sent to instruct them in the knowledge of things, none had ever appeared; and to entreat that some such men might soon be sent among them to teach them writing, reading and other things. Their lordships dismissed them well pleased, with assurances of

representing to the king the subjects of
their talk. His majesty was soon after
graciously pleased to order them a variety of presents, and to direct that particular care should be taken for their safe return to their own country. The tavern-
keeper and the Jew, who had made a
show of them, were brought before a
great assembly, and severely reprimand-
ed. On the third of March the chiefs em-
barked on board a ship in the Thames on
their return home."

[Page 212.]

The desire for education has followed
all branches of the Cherokee Tribe. Re-
becca Harding Davis found the same desire among the Eastern Cherokees, as is
seen in her article "By-paths in the
Mountains"* in which she writes :—

"Our friends found the Nation hidden
in isolated huts in the thickets among the
ravines of the Saco and Ownolafta hills.
These Cherokees number about fifteen
hundred souls and were said to have ten
thousand acres under cultivation. But
there was no sign of a village, no school,
no gathering place of any kind; the
grass was knee-deep before the door of

*Harper's Magazine, 1880.

the little church, which they had built
years ago. Not far from it is the grave
of six hundred warriors buried centuries
ago. They still bury their dead
under great heaps of stones. The
universal lethargy of these drowsing
mountains has probably fallen too heavily on these savages for them to be civilized; yet oddly enough they are the only
mountaineers who want to be awakened
out of their sleep. They crowded out of
every hut about the mules of the travel-
lers, begging not for money, but for
teachers. These strangers were the
"North" to them, and the North to the
Indians, as to the blacks in the South, is
a great magician, who can give money,
life—what it will. "My people," said
Enola, the preacher, "have lived in these
hills since before the whiteman came to
this country, and have asked for nothing
but schools; but they have never got
them." The tribe are wretchedly poor;
swindlers found the red man as easy a
prey in North Carolina as in the West,
and it is only since 1875 that they have
obtained possession of the land on which
they have lived for more than five hundred years."

[Selected from Indian Myths.]

The Cherokee Indian relates that a number of beings were employed in constructing the sun, which planet was made first. It was the intention of the Creators that men should live always; but the sun having surveyed the land, and finding an insufficiency for their support, changed the design, and arranged that they should die. The daughter of the sun was first to suffer under the law. She was bitten by a serpent and died. Thereupon the sun decreed that man should live always. At the same time he commissioned a few persons to take a box and seek the spirit of his daughter, and return with it encased therein. In no wise must the box be opened. Immortality fled, men must die.

It is affirmed by the Cherokee Indians that fire was believed an intermediate spirit, nearest the sun. A child was waved over the fire immediately after its birth; its guardianship was entreated for children. Hunters waved their moccasins over it for protection against the bite of serpents. They speak of it as an active and intelligent being. Some people of this tribe of Indians represent fire as having been born or brought with them. Oth-

ers that they sent for it to the man of fire
across immense waters, and a spider was
commissioned to answer their prayers.
On its web was brought the mystic fire;
but alas! enemies captured it, and it was
lost; yet a certain portion remains inside
the earth, from which the new fire at the
sacred feast of First Fruits is made.

INDEX,

—o—

Adair, 33.

Adair, Dr. W. T., 213.

Advocate, xiv, 129, 130, 145, 149, 190, 214.

Ah-yo-keh, 101.

Alphabet, 110, 112, 148.

Algier cited, 33, 34, 163.

A. B. C. F. M., 33, 35, 124 145, 235.

Annual Register, (Dodsley.) 14, 237.

Arch, John 113.

Armstrong, 220.

At-see, 113.

Bailey, L. D., xiv.

Bartlett S. C. 143.

Benge, John 226.

Bibles, 3, 110, 169.

Big Half Breed, 42,

Boudinot, Elias 129, 151.

Boudinot, E. C. 128.

Boudinot, W. P. xvi, 71, 130, 147.

Boot, The 118, 119.

Brainerd, 126.

Brown, Catherine 125.

Brown, David. 124, 125, 151.

Bushyhead, D. W. 179—182.

Bushyhead, Jesse 179.

Butrick, 117, 124.

Chamberlin, A. N. 107, 110, 214.

Civil War, 145—146.

Chungke 58.

Corn Dance 57.

Cornwall, 128.

Council House, 177.

Colton's Indians, cited, 38 47, 54, 71.

Collections of Georgia, 52 86.

Couch, Nevada 124.

Crawling Snake, 42

Davis, R. H. quoted, 229, 239.

Dodge, R. I., cited, 31. 32.

Dodge, J. R. quoted, 21, 63.

Drake, cited, 139.

Duncan, W. A., xiii, 166, 204, 226.

Ebenezer, 8, 10, 13, 14.

Father of Life, 40.

Gallatin, quoted 104, 105.

Gist, George, 13 16, 20, 22, 25.

Geo. II. 4, 14.

Georgia Laws, 139—142.

Goldsmith, quoted, 11.
Gould, Hattie 128.
Griffin, 107,
Harpers Magazine quoted
  26, 30 35, 42, 103 229,
  234. See Phillips.
Hicks, Chas. 42, 43, 119.
Hill, Rev. T., xvii.
Hymns, 3, 154,
Indian Letter Book, 112,
  169.
Irving, quoted, 19, 31.
Jews, 16, 53.
Johnson, Geo. 130.
Jones, C. C. xiv, cited, 5,
  8, 10, 41, 55.
Ke-a-ha-ta-kee, 16.
Longfellow quoted, 41,
  44, 73, 217.
Lord's Prayer, 111.
Lowrey, 46, 104.
Luther, Martin, 3, 4.
Marriage, 16. 68, 203.
Medal, 126, 176.
McKinney, T. L. 60, 69.
Missionary Herald, 53.
  108, 114.
Monmouth, wreck of, 144
Morehouse, Rev. H. xvi.
Moravians. 42, 43 93.
Nuntayalee, 113.
Occonnostota, 224, 226.
Pathkiller, 42, 118.
Phillips, 26, 30, 35, 36,
  37, 42, 43, 101.

Phœnix, 94, 127, 128, 128
  131, 141, 142.
Printing established, 127
Ramsey, quoted, 15, 19, 58
Refuge, city of, 16.
Ridge, Major 66,
Riley, Major, 42.
Rising Fawn, 42.
Ross, Chief, 126, 144, 175.
Ross. W. P., 130.
Ross, D. H., 130.
Scandal, laws on, 135.
Sign Boards, 130.
Societies, 2, 6, 176, 207.
Spotted Snake, Speech of,
  135.
St. Clair, 91.
Stewart, D. 89.
Stone, B. H., xvi.
Torrey, C. C. 26.
Tobacco and pipes, 33, 49.
Trademark, 43.
Traditions, 52, 56.
Walker quoted, 221.
Washington, Gen. 91, 42.
Washington, trip to, 150
War Song, 61.
Whittier, xiv. quoted, 5,
  18, 36.
Willstown, 120.
Worcester, S. A 106, 130.
Worcester, Academy 124.
Vann, James 130.
Visions, 33, 159, 162.